MISSION OF FEAR

MISSION OF FEAR

George Harmon Coxe

Originally published in 1962.

Published by Wildside Press, LLC.
Visit us online at wildsidepress.com

INTRODUCTION
KARL WURF

George Harmon Coxe (1901–1984) was one of the most prolific and widely read American mystery writers of the mid-20th century, best known for his hard-edged protagonists, rapid pacing, and unpretentious style. With a background in journalism, Coxe brought a brisk, unsentimental tone to his fiction that appealed to readers of pulp magazines and mass-market paperbacks alike. He published more than sixty novels and countless short stories, many of which first appeared in legendary pulps like *Black Mask* and *Detective Fiction Weekly*.

Coxe's breakthrough came in the 1930s with the creation of Kent Murdock, a crime-solving news photographer who blended tough-guy instincts with a pressman's eye for detail. Murdock was a deliberate evolution from Coxe's earlier character, Flashgun Casey, who also worked behind a camera and became the basis for *Casey, Crime Photographer*, a long-running radio series. The formula Coxe developed—an amateur sleuth who understands both the criminal underworld and the mechanisms of justice—would influence generations of American detective fiction.

Though not as flamboyantly stylized as Dashiell Hammett or Raymond Chandler, Coxe occupied an important middle ground between the lean prose of classic hardboiled fiction and the more procedural, psychologically driven mysteries of the postwar period. His stories often hinge on seemingly small details that spiral into deadly consequences—plots in which mistaken identities, hidden pasts, and social respectability come into sharp, often ironic conflict.

Coxe's work is also notable for its emphasis on professionalism. His protagonists are not adventurers or eccentrics but men who approach crime-solving through their trades—whether in news, photography, or business. This lends a credibility and groundedness to his narratives, placing them firmly in the everyday realities of mid-century American life.

For readers who enjoy *Mission of Fear*, several other novels offer equally compelling mysteries in Coxe's signature style. *The Man Who Died Twice* explores the tangled motives behind a supposed suicide. *The Groom Lay Dead* is a crisp whodunit set against the backdrop of a society wedding gone wrong. And *Broken Image* delivers a tightly plotted tale of murder and scandal in the world of tabloid journalism.

Coxe may not have sought literary fame, but his steady, disciplined story-telling earned him a permanent place in the history of American crime fiction. His novels remain refreshingly direct, surprisingly dark, and deeply satisfying to this day.

CHAPTER 1

THE FIRST WORD JOHN Hayden heard about the stranger who had arrived in Morrisville to threaten his marriage came from Lee Cramer, who ran the filling station at the south edge of the village. It was a gray, damp, and windy day in early March, with no promise of spring in the raw air, and now, at five-thirty, it was nearly dark when Hayden, on his way home from his small factory near South Norwalk, angled the sedan into the service area and stopped opposite the row of gasoline pumps.

There were no other customers and Cramer popped out of the concrete cube which was his office and hurried forward, leaning a little against the wind and giving a tug to the zipper on the short woolen jacket he wore over his coveralls. He was a short but sturdy man with a rugged face and a lively manner, and as Hayden rolled the window down, Cramer remarked with some disgust that it was a lovely day. Hayden said yes but at least it was a change, it wasn't raining.

"Fill it up?"

"Please. I think the front end is okay for now."

Cramer activated the pump's motor, and with the nozzle inserted and the automatic cutoff working, he picked a paper towel from the dispensing container, squirted cleaner on one side of the windshield, and began to polish it. He had finished half of this when he stopped and looked at Hayden.

"Say, did that fellow find your place all right yesterday afternoon?"

"What fellow?" Hayden said, leaning toward the open window.

"He drove in here and asked if there was a good motel in town." Cramer walked around the hood and attacked the remaining part of the windshield. "I told him The Shady Maple was the only one we had, and then he asked if I knew you. I told him yes. I said you were a regular here and he asked how to get to your place. I told him."

"Did he give his name?"

"I didn't ask him."

"What did he look like?"

Cramer heard the cutoff work in the nozzle and disappeared behind the car to remove it. When he had racked it in place and stopped the motor he said: "Three-eighty, Mr. Hayden. I'll get the book."

When he came out of the office with the charge book, Hayden repeated the question.

"Oh—average size, dark-haired, late thirties maybe. A snappy dresser with a city look to him. The cocky type. Nosy too."

"Oh? What did he say?"

"He said he was a friend of yours. Wanted to know if you didn't have a factory that made citizen-band radios, and when I said yes, he asked how you were doing. By then I'd had enough. I told him if he was a friend of yours he could ask you himself. He said he would. That's why I mentioned it to you in the first place. I thought he was going to look you up."

Hayden signed the book and stepped on the starter, a frown working at his brown eyes as he tried to place someone who would fit Cramer's description. When he failed he thanked Cramer for the information and drove down the main street toward Jerry's Tavern to get his nightly after-work quick one.

In other days, before he had married and moved to Morrisville, he had commuted to a small apartment not far from the Greenwich station. Like so many of his fellow travelers, he had stopped at the Commodore or the Biltmore Men's Bar to fortify himself with two martinis for the ride home. Since the habit was strong and since Marion seldom wanted but one cocktail before dinner, it was his custom on weekdays to stop at Jerry's for that first drink to lessen the tensions of his work day and bring him home for his drink with his wife in a more relaxed and human frame of mind.

Jerry's Tavern was almost directly across the street from The Shady Maple, a long, narrow, dimly lighted establishment that was part of an old building which had been sandwiched in between the more modern structures making up the rest of the block. The ancient and massive bar, the ornate back-bar, the woodwork, and the wide but uneven board floors suggested that it had always been a tavern, but under the present owner the kitchen had been modernized, so that Jerry could offer a so-called businessman's lunch as well as dinner from an à la carte menu.

John Hayden parked opposite the tavern and fifty feet short of the motel office, which stood at the head of one of the two long rectangular buildings that housed the twenty-two units, noting as he did so that perhaps a dozen cars had been parked aslant in the quadrangle. He considered again the information given him by Lee Cramer as he crossed the wide, tree-lined village street, wondering some but not bothered as he entered the tavern and angled toward the familiar bar.

Jerry himself was presiding, as he usually did at this hour, a large and beefy man with a round balding head and very little neck. He wore white half-sleeved shirts winter and summer, thereby exposing a pair of hard and hairy forearms that tapered only slightly to his massive and formidable fists. Now, seeing Hayden enter, he reached for a bottle of bourbon, dropped ice cubes into an Old-Fashioned glass, added whisky and a twist of lemon.

"Evening, Mr. Hayden," he said as he centered the glass and picked up the dollar bill. "When do you think we'll see the sun again?"

"What are the odds?"

"Prohibitive."

Jerry punched the cash register, put change on the bar, and moved away to draw a beer for another customer. Hayden took a sip of his drink and turned with one elbow on the bar to inspect the interior. He was a rangy-looking man of thirty-two, with good height and no more weight problem than he had when he was running the hurdles for the small Ohio university where he got his education. His dark brown hair matched his eyes, his brows were straight, his jaw angular but well cut beneath a wide mouth that was quick to smile and made one forget his face was a little gaunt to be handsome.

The smile came when his glance looked past the customers at the bar and he saw Doris Lamar give him a small and welcoming salute as she moved from the kitchen and began to set dinner places for a couple at one of the booths that stretched along the opposite wall. He did not recognize the pair, or the second couple who occupied the booth at the rear, but he took time to give his approval to the nicely rounded and supple body of the waitress as she went so efficiently about her work. It was as he turned back to his drink that he noticed George Freeman at the far end of the bar.

Freeman was the acting manager of The Shady Maple while the owner and his wife were spending three months in Florida, a stubby pleasant-mannered man of forty or so, with a colorless and inconspicuous look that seemed somehow to present exactly the proper appearance for the job he performed. Hayden did not know him well, but he had heard that Freeman had become romantically inclined toward Doris in the past months. Now, sitting hunched over the bar on his solitary stool, there was a look of acute melancholia on his round, boyish face, and the dark glasses he wore seemed strangely out of place, considering the hour and time of year.

Because his attitude seemed so out of character, Hayden wondered about it as he took another sip of his drink. For Freeman was normally a friendly person in a shy sort of way, and to watch him when Doris was present, to see the way his eyes followed her about, was to know that he was very fond of her indeed. Even when he was talking to someone else, his approving glance sought her out, and his smile was quick and eager and obvious whenever he caught her eye. There was, somehow, a worshipful quality in that look, and the regulars who understood the relationship would wink and grin when they noticed it. But this was a different man. This was a sullen, brooding man, and when Doris came to get refills for the couple in the rear booth, Hayden's curiosity got the better of him.

"What's the matter with the boy friend?"

"Scotch and water and another daiquiri, Jerry," she said before she acknowledged the question. "Hello, Mr. Hayden. You mean George? He's sulking tonight."

"Why the dark glasses?"

"He had a little accident."

"Today?"

"Last night."

"From you?"

"From the fellow I was with."

She did not look at him when she spoke but watched her tray, and when the drinks were ready she went away. As she did so, George Freeman slipped from his stool and started for the door. Looking neither to the right nor the left, and acknowledging no one's presence, he marched out, and it was then that Hayden noticed the discoloration under one eye that the dark glasses could not quite hide.

Jerry, who had moved opposite Hayden, watched Freeman's stiff-legged exit and muttered softly.

"I asked him if he ran into a door and he said no."

"Who's the fellow Doris mentioned?"

"Never saw him before. Came in yesterday about this time. Had a few drinks and then dinner. He was kidding around with Doris and I guess she and George had had a tiff or something because she had her back up and went along with the kidding."

"Was Freeman here?"

"Sure. That's the reason she was putting on the act if you ask me. He stood here glowering for a while and when he couldn't take it any longer he went over to the table and they had some words and George took off. That's all I knew about it until this guy shows up at ten when Doris is getting through and drives off with her."

He went away to serve another bar customer and Hayden, sensing some movement beside him, turned to find the girl at his side. She seemed at ease now that Freeman had gone and her green eyes beneath the penciled brows appraised him as she touched her hair to see if the curled ends at the back of her neck were all in place. It was blond hair, a chemical job but well done, and he decided it suited the rest of her face, which was perhaps a bit too coarse in some features to be pretty but attractive for all that if one overlooked the permanent aging at the corners of the mouth and the disillusionment that was mirrored in her eyes. About thirty he thought, or a bit more, but this light was very kind to her and he could understand why men might be attracted to her.

"I thought you and Freeman had things worked out."

"Not quite, Mr. Hayden."

"I had the idea you liked him."

"I do. But he doesn't own me. Not yet anyway. And I didn't start that business last night; he did." She made a small, deprecating sound and a corner of her mouth dipped. "He's forty but I guess he hasn't been around women much because there's an awful lot he doesn't know. Why he was even jealous of you."

"Me?" Hayden said in quick astonishment.

"Because you drove me home that rainy night a week or so ago."

Hayden remembered the night. He had worked late and stopped in about nine-thirty for one drink. Business was slack and he asked Doris if she had a ride and she said no, so he drove her to the small cottage she had rented, a three-block ride that lasted little more than three minutes.

"George stopped here a little after ten that night," she added, "and Jerry told him he'd let me off early. It took George all the next day to stop sulking. When he went into the same routine last night just because he thought I was being too friendly to a customer, I decided to show him he couldn't tell me what to do."

"Jerry said he was a stranger."

"He was, and if George hadn't made such a fuss I probably wouldn't have gone out with Sam later. Not that there was anything wrong with him. He was not bad-looking, the city type, a sharp dresser. You could tell he'd been around but then"—she tipped her head and gave him a lopsided smile—"so have I. I've seen a lot of Sam Adlers. Cocky, good spenders, always on the make for one thing or another. Hard to discourage but not hard to handle once you understand what makes them tick.

"After George had made his little scene and I finally got rid of him, I decided to teach him a lesson and Sam made it easy. He asked when I got off and I told him. He said would I like to go somewhere later for a drink and a dance and I said maybe I would. He picked me up at ten and we went to the Log Cabin," she added, mentioning a run-of-the-mill night spot on the Post Road. "George must have followed us because he came storming up to the table and tried to get tough. Sam was agreeable. George swung but Sam beat him to the punch and the owner escorted George to the door. Poor George," she said and then, as a new thought occurred to her, the green eyes sobered.

"Incidentally, Sam asked about you."

The statement reminded Hayden of the information Lee Cramer had given him at the gasoline station and suddenly an odd and unaccountable feeling of uneasiness started to work inside him. A frown dug in above the bridge of his nose and the brown eyes narrowed slightly as he studied her.

"You say his name was Sam Adler?"

"That's the name he gave me."

"What did he look like?"

He listened carefully as she gave her description, and the picture that came to him corresponded with the one Cramer had drawn. To this Doris added a thought of her own.

"He gave me the idea he was some sort of business acquaintance, but if you ask me you'd be more likely to find him at the race track than you would in an office."

Hayden finished his drink and put the glass down, the uneasiness expanding and his thoughts uncertain. Sam Adler, whoever he was, had been in town since yesterday afternoon and he knew where the Haydens lived. But Marion had said nothing about receiving a caller yesterday. So maybe Adler hadn't called yesterday. Maybe he'd called today.

He tried to remember whether his wife's manner and actions had been any different when he came home last night and remembered now that there had been one small change. She had had a drink before he came in last night and this in itself was unusual. But he understood that women who were four months pregnant were likely to do unusual things now and then, and he had not given it a second thought. Now, aware that there was no point in letting his imagination get off the track, he knew that it was time to go home. He glanced at his watch, thanked the girl for the information, and, in the act of turning away, stopped abruptly.

"Have you seen him since last night?"

"Yes. He was in for lunch. He's staying over at The Shady Maple if you want to talk to him. Room twelve."

Hayden thanked her again. He said maybe he would talk to Adler, but not now. He went out quickly then, his bony face somber and signs of worry beginning to show in the dark brown eyes.

CHAPTER 2

JOHN HAYDEN KNEW AS he walked into the living room of the ranch-style home they had bought six months earlier that something was definitely wrong; he knew it even before he saw his wife and the empty Old-Fashioned glass on the end table beside the wing chair.

He had parked the sedan next to the station wagon that Marion used to run around in and had come through the small breezeway to the kitchen. The door to the dining room area at the end of the living room was open and the lights were on but there was no sound and this in itself was disturbing. Always before, she was waiting for him in the kitchen by the time he had parked the car and always, even when she did not feel well, there was a smile and a kiss for him, a moment when she stood close when his arms tightened about her.

Before that, in the rented house where they had spent their first eight months of married life, there was not even a garage and she somehow always managed to hear him arrive and meet him at the door. Now he saw the ice bucket and the bottle of whisky and the steak which had been put out to defrost; the potatoes, which had been scrubbed for baking, were still on the counter and the oven had not yet been turned on.

"Marion?"

There was no answer as he crossed to the open door and he called again, his voice carrying an edge that worry and anxiety had put there. He was in the other room then, hurrying a little until he saw her in the chair, the light from the floor lamp burnishing her soft dark hair. Even then there was no reaction until he stopped in front of her.

"Oh, hello," she said, not looking at him.

"Hi, darling."

He bent down to kiss her and she turned her head slightly, so that his lips found a cheek that was soft, fragrant, and discouragingly cold. He straightened slowly, greatly disturbed now and a little scared. It took an effort to contain himself and he did not know whether to sit down and ask for some explanation or pretend that he was not yet aware that anything was wrong.

Because he wanted to give her a chance to make the first move, he kept his tone unconcerned.

"Hey," he said lightly. "You've already had a drink."

"You always stop for one at the tavern, don't you?"

"Sure, sure."

"So what's wrong with me having one too if I want it?"

"Nothing, sweetheart. Just making an observation. I'll fix a fresh one."

"Do that," she said. "I think you're going to need it. And make another one for me, a strong one, please."

"Right." He leaned down to take her glass. "Shall I turn the oven on?"

"Oven?" she said, as though she had never heard the word before.

"For the potatoes. Do you want me to put them in now?"

"If you want to."

By the time he had reached the kitchen he was thoroughly upset and he stood a moment by the sink and let his breath out slowly. Somewhere in the back of his mind was the thought of a stranger named Sam Adler, but he could not yet accept the intuitive prodding that told him this man might be the key to his wife's strange conduct. Instead his glance moved idly about the modern room and he recalled how delighted Marion had been when they first inspected the house. The owner, who had built it two years earlier, had been transferred by his company to the Pittsburgh office, and they had been lucky to get something that suited them so well at a fair price.

Now, seeing again the scrubbed potatoes and the built-in oven, he decided to ignore them. When he went to the refrigerator to get a lemon he noticed the row of gleaming copper pans on the pegboard at one side of the stove. They came in graduated sizes and Marion treated them as though they were heirlooms made of some precious metal. The knife that he usually used to cut lemon peel was not in the rack but he had no wish to look for it and he used the next size, cutting generous slices and bruising them against the bottoms of the Old-Fashioned glasses with the end of a mixing spoon before adding water and bitters and sugar, a pinch for him, a more generous portion for her. He cracked ice, added whisky, stirred, and still he stood there until he was sure he could face her with his thoughts and emotions under control.

She had not moved while he was in the kitchen, and when he had put her drink on the end table, he took the chair which faced hers from the other side of the fireplace. He took a cigarette from the silver box beside him, not offering her one because she had stopped smoking when her pregnancy was confirmed. When he had a light he said: "Cheers, dear," and pretended not to notice when there was no reply.

He took a big swallow and the whisky put a welcome warmth in his throat and the top of his stomach. He let the silence build as he studied her, and though she still would not look at him he saw that her cheekbones, which to him had always added some extra beauty to her face, were pale now, the smooth skin taut-looking, the full, sweetly shaped mouth compressed and severe. The hazel eyes were fastened on her glass, but he could see the long black lashes, unblinking now and fixed by some inner struggle that was tormenting her. She was wearing a flannel skirt and cashmere sweater set, and it came to him now that she did not look four months pregnant.

She denied this when he had mentioned the subject before. She said her clothes were beginning to feel too tight but he could only be sure at night when, under the gentleness of his hand, he could feel the rounded firmness beneath the satiny skin of her belly that grew so gradually from week to week. He had told her that she must tell him when the first signs of life came, so he could feel it for himself, and she had promised him that she would....

He pulled his thoughts back to the moment and a sickness began to grow inside him as he tried to make his voice hearty.

"Have a tough day, baby?"

"You could call it that."

"Any morning sickness after I left?"

"Some."

"Has Junior been behaving?"

"Junior's been fine," she said in the same dull tones. "Unfortunately—" She stopped here; then, as though becoming aware of the glass in her hand for the first time, she lifted it and he could see her throat move as she took two quick swallows. She put the glass down on the end table and the sound of it was loud in the otherwise quiet room. But she was looking at him now, her chin up, the stiffness still in her face, her eyes enormous. He saw her lips quiver once and then she said harshly: "Unfortunately for Junior, he's going to be a bastard."

He heard the phrase distinctly but he did not believe his ears, and for that first shocking instant he was more distressed by the word itself than by the inference it conveyed. The effect was more punishing than a physical blow because it struck deep inside him and he had as yet no time to consider her meaning or speculate about the reasons for her outburst. For one of the first things that had attracted him to her was a look of breeding that he had found authentic, and in their fourteen months of married life the closest Marion had ever come to profanity was three or four determined damns, and then only under extreme provocation.

True, in the past couple of months there had been small emotional up-
heavals, but he understood that these were due to her condition and he made
the proper allowances. He knew that she felt queasy at times, that morning
sickness bothered her now and then. There were occasional tears that seemed
to have no logical explanation, but if she was sometimes a bit difficult she
could also be contrite; when the outbursts were over, the proof of her feeling
of guilt was often demonstrated by a passion that surprised him. All these
thoughts came to him as he stared at her, and before he could demonstrate or
reply she attacked him again.

"Did you hear what I said?"

"I heard you."

"Well, say something. Or do you want me to repeat it?"

It came to him then that she was trying to tell him something that he was in
no condition mentally or emotionally to accept. This was no outburst brought
about by some instability of the mind. He knew somehow that she was close
to hysteria and such knowledge chilled him and put a further strain on nerves
already ragged. He wanted to come out of the chair and shake her, to shout at
her to stop this nonsense, but some inner warning signal made him sit still
and demand an explanation as soberly as he could.

"Not now or any other time," he said, an edge in his tone. "Just give a simple
explanation of what you're talking about—if you can."

The cold, no-nonsense quality of the words had their effect, and he saw her
labored breath as she fought for some self-control. He watched it, the slow
gathering of that control, and her voice, when it came, was as distant as his
own.

"A child whose parents are not married is illegitimate. If you prefer that
word, let's use it. All I'm trying to say is that our baby will be illegitimate."

"What?" He felt the back of his neck prickle as he sat up, and suddenly his
scalp was tight. "What the devil are you talking about? You must be—"

"But I'm not," she said, interrupting. "I found out today that we're not
married, at least not legally."

"*Marion!*"

"No." She gestured impatiently with one hand. "Let me finish, please. It's
really very simple. Ted is still alive."

He knew what she meant then but he could not accept the statement.
His mind and senses rebelled and he fought against belief, even though he
knew that for her there could be but one Ted. He himself had never seen the
man—Marion had been widowed for six months when he first met her—but
he knew that for a period of three years she had been Mrs. Ted Corbin.

"I don't believe it," he said, aware of the inadequacy of his words but unable to find others.

"I didn't want to believe it either but it's true. I saw his picture—"

A sob that was a convulsive choking sound cut through the sentence and he saw her face crumble. Tears spilled from her eyes. When she could no longer face him she bowed her head and covered her mouth and eyes with her hands. The sight of all this torment and helplessness chewed his insides and he came to his feet with a muffled curse. Two long strides took him to her chair and he went to one knee and leaned close.

In his effort to comfort her he took her hands and pulled them gently down and she did not resist. He started to slide an arm around her shoulders and draw her close, and suddenly he could feel her stiffen. When he tried to persist she drew back. Her head came up, and though her eyes were still wet, they were wide open now and there was a look in them he had never seen before. Then, as the astonishment grew in him, she put her hands against his chest and pushed.

"Don't touch me."

"Marion!"

"I mean it."

The cold and brittle sound of the words told him that she was deadly serious, and although he did not understand what prompted the outburst, he wisely withdrew his arm and came to his feet.

He went back to his chair, glaring now as he saw his drink. He snatched it up and finished it in one gulp, but this time the whisky did him no good. For the anger was rising in him now, an impotent helpless anger that had no direction. It took a considerable effort for him to sit down and face her again, to see that the tears had stopped and that she was frightened by what she had done.

"Who told you?" he demanded.

"A man."

It seemed then, as he recalled the information he had picked up at Cramer's filling station and Jerry's Tavern, that he already had the answer.

"Was his name Adler?"

The question seemed to startle her. "How—how did you know?"

"When was the first time you saw him, yesterday afternoon?"

He had her attention now. Her lips were parted and she moistened them with the tip of her tongue. She sat up a little straighter, the hazel eyes puzzled and all traces of hysteria gone.

"But—how did you know, John?"

He told her. He spoke of Lee Cramer and Doris Lamar and George Freeman. He kept his voice level in an effort to mask his own doubt and anxiety.

"Yes," she said when he repeated his question. "I guess it was around four."

"Did you let him in?"

"No. I hadn't finished dressing. I had the chain lock on the front door like I always do when you're not here. He said he was a book salesman. I told him I didn't want any and he asked me if I had any children. I said no."

"Then what?"

"He said he was selling some sort of encyclopedia for children. He seemed pleasant enough and I didn't want to be rude so"—she hesitated and sounded a bit embarrassed as she continued—"I don't know why I told him this but—"

"Never mind why. Just tell me what you said."

"I told him there might be a child in another five months and if he wanted to come around again after that I might consider his proposition." She hesitated again, a frown working on the smoothness of her brow and worry once more clouding her glance. "I started to close the door and he put his weight against it. He gave me a funny smile and suddenly I was afraid of him. I told him if he didn't leave I would call the police and he said that would be all right with him. He said he wasn't really selling books; he just wanted to get a look at me. He said he had a message from my husband."

Again she stopped and once more Hayden prompted her. "What did you say?"

"I told him he was being ridiculous, that if I wanted to talk to my husband all I had to do was pick up the telephone. He said he didn't mean my present husband; he meant Ted Corbin."

She took a small breath and said: "I don't know what all I said then. I know I told him I didn't believe him, that Ted had been killed along with fifty-eight other people in a plane crash more than two years ago. I guess I said some other things and he waited until I finished, that sly look still in his eyes and that half-smile on his mouth. Then he told me I was mistaken. He said he had seen Ted two weeks ago, that he was in perfect health.

"'I can prove it to you Mrs. Corbin,' he said. 'Or Mrs. Hayden, if you like it better that way. Suppose we keep it a secret, just the two of us, until to-morrow. I'll be back tomorrow afternoon and I'll bring that proof with me. If you're smart you'll listen to the proposition I have in mind.'"

Again she ran out of breath and this time she stopped. She continued to look right at him but it seemed to him that she did not really see him and after another moment he stood up, the glass still in his hand.

"I take it he came back this afternoon."

"Yes."

"With proof?"

"He showed me a snapshot of Ted."

"It could have been taken a long time ago."

"That's what I told him but I knew it wasn't so. Ted's alive."

There were a lot of things he wanted to say then but he knew they could wait. He saw that his wife's drink had scarcely been touched, and now, as he stopped beside her chair, he took the handkerchief from his breast pocket and passed it to her.

"Blow your nose." He waited until she took the handkerchief. "And work on that drink a little, will you?"

"I don't want it."

"Pretend it's medicine. We've got some talking to do," he said. "I want to hear more about this proof Adler has. I want to know just what happened this afternoon."

He moved through the dining room area to the kitchen door and stopped to glance back at her. He said he was going to make another drink and while he was doing it she could try to remember exactly what had been said.

CHAPTER 3

JOHN HAYDEN DID NOT make a fresh Old-Fashioned but simply added ice and whisky to the dregs of the first one. He gave the mixture a quick and violent stir. When he had tossed the spoon aside he did not lift the glass but stood staring with unseeing eyes at the darkness outside the windows while he tried to ease the tension inside him and quiet his trembling nerves.

He held one hand out palm down and watched his fingers shake. When he could not still them he clenched his fist and shifted his glance. Again he noticed the steak, and because he knew it would not be cooked tonight, he put it back into the refrigerator and tossed the potatoes into the vegetable bin. The diversion helped and his breathing was all right now but there was some thinking to be done and it came to him that this was the time to do it.

He had to think logically, reasonably, sensibly, and he was afraid he could not do so while sitting opposite Marion and watching the naked display of emotions on her sensitive face. To see and understand her distress was to undermine his own self-control and involve him emotionally as well, and this would only further erode his own resolve to find the truth as soon as possible.

To set the pattern he directed his mind deliberately to the accident which had taken Ted Corbin's life more than two years ago. At the time the name meant nothing to him and he had not yet met Marion, but the accident was a front-page story, not only because of the lives lost, but because the mid-air disintegration of the aircraft was so similar to an accident that had happened some months before.

He had left New York and was working for Brandt Radio and Electronics Company at the time and later, when he met Marion, he remembered the accounts he had read. At first there was some talk of sabotage because the destruction of the aircraft was complete and parts of it, as well as bodies and parts of bodies, had been scattered over a wide area of the farm land on which they fell. Later, the experts were able to determine that the disaster was caused not by sabotage but by some structural failure which, combined with the air pressure at thirty-two thousand feet, had produced the explosive effect.

He learned other details while he was courting Marion. She had already been widowed for six months when he met her at a party in Greenwich, and it was another six months before they were married. The accident had not been mentioned since, but he remembered now that Ted Corbin had gone to Illinois, ostensibly on business but actually to look for a new job. He had gone aboard this particular flight at Capitol City one evening, and about an hour out, somewhere over Indiana, tragedy had struck the plane, its crew, and its passengers.

Because of the violence of the accident, identification had been difficult in many instances; in some it had been impossible. As a result the remains of certain passengers known to have been aboard the aircraft had been buried in a common grave. Ted Corbin was one of these. He had been an orphan who had no living relatives, and Marion, in no condition to consider the grisly evidence, had taken the advice of friends and approved the arrangement.

There had been some insurance involved—a small life policy that Corbin had carried for some time, plus a seventy-five-thousand-dollar trip policy he had bought in the airport. The fact that the insurance company had paid this claim seemed proof enough that Ted Corbin did indeed die aboard that aircraft. It was this fact that now came to bolster Hayden's contention that Corbin was dead and that Sam Adler's scheme, whatever it was, could not be based on fact. Such thoughts helped as he picked up his glass and started for the living room.

Knowing nothing at all about the proof his wife had spoken about, he understood that she was convinced that Sam Adler had told the truth. He was willing to let matters stand that way for the present because it seemed more important to reassure her about the baby and make her understand that her fears were exaggerated, that the conclusion she had reached was subject to sensible revision. Once he had explained things to her, he could go on to the details of her talk with Adler and see just what had to be done.

"You spoke about proof," he said as he sat down, "but let's skip that for now." He put his glass aside and fashioned a smile for her. "Come on, baby, take another sip of your drink."

He waited, pleased and encouraged when she took a small and dutiful swallow.

"Okay," he said. "Now, before you tell me just what happened this afternoon, let's get one thing straight." He paused again, his dark eyes intent. "Junior is not going to be illegitimate except in a very technical sense and probably not even that."

"But if Ted is alive—"

"Please! Let me finish. If he *is* alive, and I'm not buying that yet, you have plenty of grounds for a quick and quiet divorce that no one around here has to know about. You can do that in Nevada or Alabama or Mexico. We can be remarried just as quietly. So if we can do that, how can the baby be illegitimate?"

"Are you sure?" she said, hope touching her glance for the first time.

He was not at all sure and knew little about such laws, but he also knew there would be some way out and he lied convincingly.

"Certainly I'm sure. So let's forget about that angle and talk about this guy Adler. He says Ted Corbin is alive and I say he isn't. I wasn't there at the time, but you and Roger Denham went out west after the accident. You know the facts; you told them to me. Corbin wired you that he would be on that flight. The airline people said he was checked aboard, didn't they?"

"Yes."

"They found his trench coat and figured this had been hanging in the tail compartment, which explained why it wasn't burned. You identified that trench coat. The name tape you had sewn in it was still there. The baggage check they gave him when he handed in his ticket was in the pocket. They found his suitcase. Part of it was charred but there was enough still intact for you to identify his toilet kit and a pair of his shoes."

"Yes, but—"

"Furthermore," he went on, not to be interrupted, "the insurance companies never pay off until they are convinced the claim is justified. So let's get back to Adler."

He sat up, aware that he had her attention now, that all traces of hysteria had gone. "He came here yesterday afternoon and talked to you. He came back this afternoon and you let him in."

"I had to. I had to find out the truth, didn't I? I'd thought about nothing else for twenty-four hours. I was scared but I tried not to show it. I told him the same things you've just told me and he just nodded, and smiled in that sly way of his, and showed me the snapshot. It was Ted."

"How do you know it hadn't been taken a long time ago?"

"I just know. He had coveralls on with some insignia on the chest. I could see a little of the background and it looked to me as if he was working in a filling station. It certainly hadn't been taken while we were married and I know he couldn't have looked like that before that. He looked older, and a little leaner, and he was bareheaded, and tanned—"

"There could be some other explanation," Hayden said. "One little snapshot isn't enough."

"He also showed me some fingerprints."

"What?" He peered at her. "What fingerprints?"

"He had a picture of the fingerprints of one hand, a photograph. He said they were Ted's fingerprints."

The statement jarred Hayden and his earlier uncertainty began to undermine his thoughts, even as he sought some way to refute this new evidence.

"How do you know they're Corbin's?" he demanded. "Those prints could be anybody's."

"Adler said he could prove it if he had to."

"How?"

"When Ted was in college he worked two summers for some government project in Tennessee. I don't know what it was but he had to be fingerprinted. He told me. Those prints would be on file somewhere with the government, wouldn't they?"

She shifted her weight as she spoke and leaned forward, her arms crossed and hugging her breasts. She was dry-eyed and serious now, and what she said then reminded him again that his wife was as intelligent as she was lovely.

"I think we should stop talking about the word *if*. Instead of doubting that Ted is alive, let's assume for a moment that he *is*."

He did not like the assumption but he was forced to admit that it had some merit.

"All right," he said. "Adler says he can prove that your husband is alive. So what's his angle? What does he want?"

"Just what you'd think he might want. Money."

"How much?"

"Twenty thousand dollars."

"And for this he gives you the picture and the fingerprints and promises to forget the whole thing."

"Something like that."

"What did you tell him?"

"I told him we didn't have that much money and we couldn't raise it. He said that would be too bad because in that case he'd have to go to the insurance company. He knows the insurance people paid me seventy-five thousand dollars. He said he thought that they'd be delighted to pay him ten thousand in order to collect seventy-five thousand. If he could prove what he says, we'd have to give the money back, wouldn't we? And how could we do that?"

Hayden let out his breath and reluctantly brought into focus the thought that heretofore had been left in the back of his mind. He tried to evade it and could not. He glanced at his drink and found that it had little attraction at the moment. To give himself time he took another cigarette and lighted it with deliberate movements.

That seventy-five thousand dollars, although he did not know she had it at the time, was the extent of Marion's dowry. She had given it to him eagerly when he had a chance to take over control of the Brandt Company after the owner had died a year ago. Without that investment he would still be a salaried employee, and while the company's credit rating was good and its banking relations sound, his own personal finances allowed little leeway....

"I'm sorry," he said, aware that she had spoken.

"I said, could we raise twenty thousand?"

"Probably."

"Do you think we should? I mean, and pay him."

"I don't know what to think."

"Could you pay the insurance company back?"

"No."

"But you could pay some of it?"

"Yes."

"Maybe they would give you some time to pay the balance." She paused, nibbling absently on her lower lip. "We could sell the house and go back to renting for a while. That would help. We could sell one of the cars, or at least get two cheaper ones."

"Don't talk like that."

"But—"

"No buts either. Not now anyway." He took a swallow of his drink and stood up, a hardness in his bony jaw and his mouth grim. "Not until I've had a little session with this guy Adler."

She straightened in her chair as he spoke and traces of alarm touched her eyes.

"Not now, John. Please. I told Roger you wouldn't until you'd talked to him."

"Roger?" The word came out in an explosive sound and his stare was both angry and incredulous as his mind digested the implication. "Roger?" he said again. "You mean you told Roger about this?"

"I had to," she said, close to tears again. "I had to talk to someone."

"Maybe you had some idea about swinging this thing yourself?"

"No, it wasn't that. Please try to understand. I intended to tell you everything. I have, haven't I? But I needed someone who could be objective. I needed advice and I knew I could trust Roger. Roger's smart and intelligent and he knows all about legal things. I wanted to get his reactions before I talked to you."

There was more but Hayden did not hear it all. He could not help feeling hurt at what she had said, but as his mind moved on, the forces that had prompted her to turn immediately to Roger Denham took on some importance. For Denham had grown up with her. He knew her long before she had married Corbin, and from bits and pieces of information that had come to Hayden over the past couple of years, he understood that Denham had at one time been a suitor. He was not at all sure that Denham approved of him, but he understood that Marion looked upon Denham as a friend who was happy to advise and help her when she needed help most.

It had been Denham to whom she had turned at the time of the accident. He had gone with her to Indiana and helped with the identification and the funeral. He had represented her with the insurance company and helped her invest the proceeds until she had turned them over to Hayden. Because of this friendship, Denham had helped in setting up the present corporate plan for the Brandt Company when Hayden took over, and he was, in fact, the company attorney.

Remembering these things now, he realized that while Marion had turned to the lawyer on some impulse born of desperation, he, John Hayden, was probably going to need a lot of this same kind of help before this matter was settled. He did not like the way she had confided in Denham before she talked to him, but he could not quarrel with her now. It was natural enough that his feelings be hurt, but that was no longer the primary consideration.

"What did Roger say?" he asked.

"About the same things you did. He didn't believe it at first. He asked if Adler had left the photograph and the print of the fingerprints and I told him no. He didn't come right out and say so, but I think he felt the same way you did about paying for Adler's silence. He said I was to tell you the whole story and not let you rush up to The Shady Maple and deal with Adler yourself."

"Did he say why?"

"Well—" She gestured emptily and dropped her glance. "He said you were a rather well-adjusted person and not particularly aggressive but that men like you, when they had the provocation and lost their heads, could be pretty violent."

"A philosopher too, hunh?"

"Please, John."

"I'm sorry," he said and meant it. "Okay, I'll see him."

She came to her feet then and for the first time there was a small smile on her mouth and a look of relief in her eyes.

"He said he'd wait in his office for your call and that he could meet you at his place after dinner if you still wanted to talk to him." She smoothed out her skirt and twisted the cardigan back into place. "You call him and I'll see about dinner."

Hayden said he would make the call but she could forget about dinner. He told her what he had done with the steak and the potatoes. He said he wasn't hungry any more; he doubted if she was either, and why not just heat up a can of soup and make a little salad?

CHAPTER 4

ROGER DENHAM LIVED IN an old Cape Cod cottage that he had bought some years earlier and remodeled. Originally there was only the gray-shingled shell and a tree-studded, hedged-in lot, but this in itself had a charm all its own, and he had preserved most of the original features when he put in the plumbing, the heating plant, and electricity. He had good taste and he had furnished the house himself, mostly with antiques, so that each room had a comfortable, lived-in look.

As a confirmed bachelor he did more or less as he pleased. There was a cleaning woman who came mornings to get his breakfast and straighten up the place. He ate dinner out most of the time and did his entertaining at one of his two clubs. On rare occasions when he gave a dinner party he had a couple come in and take complete charge of all arrangements. Now, at eight o'clock, he answered John Hayden's knock and ushered him into the low, beamed-ceilinged living room, with its hooked rugs and paneled walls, and waved him to the slip-covered divan.

"Before you say anything, John," he said, "I hope you weren't annoyed at Marion for phoning me and explaining the situation before she talked to you."

"I may have been at the time," Hayden said, "but I'm not annoyed now. It's too late for that."

"Good. You're her husband. You're the one she loves. But I've known her longer than you have. We've been friends since we were children and she needed to talk to someone who was not emotionally involved. She felt she had to have some sound objective advice and frankly I'm glad she told me. It looks as if you're both in trouble and I hope I can be of some help."

He had moved over to the fireplace as he spoke and now he turned, his back against the glowing embers, his hands clasped behind him. Standing there in his slacks and a shetland jacket, he made a trim, athletic-looking figure, an inch or so under six feet but with good shoulders and slim hips. His hair was sandy and cut short to help disguise the fact that it was thinning somewhat, his eyes were gray, and the thin-rimmed glasses helped to give his lean face an ascetic, austere expression. His upper lip was long and not given to useless smiling, and although he was at all times polite and well mannered, there was seldom any outward display of warmth or compassion. Hayden had wondered in the past whether this was due to the fact that Denham had been orphaned early and brought up strictly by his grandparents, or whether this was something that applied only to him and was a personal reaction brought about by the knowledge that while Denham had been a long-time friend of Marion's, it was he, Hayden, she had married.

It was also possible, he knew, that his opinion of Denham was somewhat unfair. There had been times in the past when the thought of that long-time relationship had brought moments of jealousy. When Marion sensed this, she not only reassured him but laughed at him. Roger, she said, had been more like a brother than a lover. The fact that he was rather handsome, brilliant, well-brought-up, and comfortably fixed had nothing to do with it. Some men, she said, regardless of their attributes, simply did not attract some girls physically. For her, Roger was one of those.

She liked him and admired him, but his attempts to establish a more ardent relationship were misplaced and he had eventually come to accept the status quo. He had not approved of her marriage to Ted Corbin, saying that they had nothing in common, and in this he was right. That he may have felt the same way about her second marriage bothered Hayden not at all, but it could explain a lack of personal warmth, either real or imaginary, where he was concerned. In any case it did not matter. It was not important and it did not affect his respect for Denham's knowledge and ability. It was this knowledge and good judgment that he needed now and he said so.

"All right," he said, "you know the facts. What do you think we should do?"

"I think we ought to talk a little. I think you'll want to go see this fellow Adler personally, but let's take a look at all sides of his proposition first. He wouldn't leave either the picture of Ted Corbin or his fingerprints with Marion, but she saw them. I think we ought to start with the assumption that Corbin actually is alive."

"I don't see how he could be."

"Neither do I. But neither do I see anyone like Adler making a pitch like this and hoping to collect if he didn't have something tangible to sell."

"So?"

"So the easiest thing would be to pay Adler, and if that's what you have in mind I could probably cut his price in half."

"How?"

"By making a threat that will stand up. No matter what you decide to do, my advice to you is to let me carry the ball. See him by all means. Find out what you can. Play along for a while. Stall. When you've learned all you can, tell him to see me."

"Then what?"

"I'll take it from there and I can talk tough if I have to. I can get a warrant for his arrest on attempted extortion. When he sees I mean business he may decide to take, say, ten thousand dollars and get clear while he can."

Hayden thought it over and did not like the conclusion that came to him. He said he had never run into blackmail before, but from what he had read, and what he had heard, he had an idea that it would be difficult to stop paying once he had started.

"What assurance would I have that Adler wouldn't hit me again next year or the year after?"

"You wouldn't have any, except his word or the threat of arrest."

"There'd be no guarantee."

"None. And there's also another angle that you may not have considered. If Corbin is alive he disappeared deliberately through some odd coincidence that had to do with that fatal flight from Capitol City. We don't have to speculate about that now; the point is that it would not be difficult for Corbin to keep track of Marion if he wanted to. For all we know, he could be behind this blackmail, with Adler nothing more than a messenger boy or collector."

This thought was a new one to Hayden and he found it doubly discouraging. He found it hard to accept too, but he could not argue with the possibility Denham suggested.

"If that's how it happens to be, I doubt if Corbin would be satisfied with one payment."

"So do I. That's something for you and Marion to decide for yourselves, but I guess you know there's only one other alternative."

"You mean bring the whole thing out into the open."

"Exactly. Prefer charges against Adler, have him arrested; let the authorities put the pressure on him. They could make him produce Corbin if he's alive, and you'd have to work it out from there. There's no fraud involved on that insurance payment, either by you or by Marion, and if you put your cards on the table—"

"I guess they'd want their money back, wouldn't they?"

"Probably. But, even so, there's an area for discussion. Could you raise seventy-five thousand dollars?"

"No."

Denham ran fingers through his thinning hair and moved sideways so that he could lean his shoulders against the mantelpiece. He took off his glasses, frowning as he held them up to the light. As he began to polish the lenses with his handkerchief he said:

"Let me review your corporate setup and see if I've got it right. You came to work for Brandt because he was getting old and wanted someone to take over the operation. You brought in this bright young genius from M.I.T. to improve the product and do your research. You got this other youngster in to handle the sales end. Before you really got operating under the new setup, Brandt died. His estate wanted to get out from under and they gave you the opportunity to take over the business. Am I right so far?"

"Yes."

"Marion gave you the seventy-five thousand from the insurance money that I had invested for her. Your engineer and your salesman raised some money on their own and you made a small public offering of stock. So the way things stand now, you own roughly thirty per cent of the shares, your two partners own fifteen per cent each and the public holds the other forty per cent. Now how much could you raise—?"

"To get the whole seventy-five thousand," Hayden cut in, "I'd have to sell out. By pledging my shares I probably could get thirty-five or forty thousand from the bank. Certainly not more than that, the way things stand."

"It might be enough to start with."

"How do you mean?"

"Well, in the first place, that insurance money was paid to Marion. She gave it to you. That stock is not jointly owned, is it?"

"No, it's in my name."

"So how's the insurance company going to get seventy-five thousand dollars out of Marion when she doesn't have it?" He lifted one hand to forestall comment and continued: "What I'm trying to say is that this could be a matter for negotiation or the courts. We could force the insurance people to sue and there would probably be a judgment of some kind. You understand I'm simply guessing at this point because I'm not up on the laws that cover such cases."

He put on his glasses and replaced the handkerchief. "But offhand I'd say that in such a situation the insurance people would be willing to negotiate. In other words, they might well be agreeable to a settlement of somewhat less than the original amount. They could most certainly get a judgment, but since in a way it would be like finding money in the street, they'd probably make some kind of a reasonable settlement rather than have the thing drag through the courts."

"I could pay them part of it," Hayden said, "if they would take notes for the balance and let me pay it off over a period of two or three years."

"That's a possibility," Denham said, "but the thing you have to decide now is how you're going to play the hand."

"Suppose the insurance people wouldn't settle?" Hayden said, persisting. "Suppose there was some way they could force me to pay up in full?"

Denham pushed away from the mantelpiece. He took a breath and shrugged. "I'm afraid that would be tough on you; Marion too. But let's not cross that bridge yet.... Where are you going?" he asked as Hayden came to his feet.

Hayden took a moment before he replied. For the anger was stirring in him again, and it helped somewhat to combat the feeling of dejection and hopelessness that had been working on him for the past couple of hours. He found himself hating this man he had not yet seen but who had come so suddenly to threaten his marriage, his happiness, and his business.

"I'm going to see Adler," he said bluntly. "I'm going to find out what the score is and if he gives me too much trouble I'll probably break his damn neck."

"Well, don't." Denham uttered a small dry laugh to show that he understood Hayden was only kidding. "If you decide you have to get tough with him, let me handle it. I've had more experience in these things, and if I have to threaten him I can make it stick. So keep your hands in your pockets. Find out all you can. Then stall. Tell him you need more time. Go home and take a couple of sleeping pills and get a good night's rest. Get in touch with me tomorrow and we'll make some plans."

He had been walking to the door with Hayden as he spoke, and when he opened it he uttered a final word of caution.

"No rough stuff, okay?" When there was no reply he added: "I'm sorry I can't offer you a drink but you know I seldom have it around unless I'm throwing a party."

Hayden said it did not matter. He said he was going to stop at the tavern and have a couple of quick brandies to settle his nerves. After that he'd see what Sam Adler had to say.

———◦◦◦———

The front of The Shady Maple Motel was well lighted at this hour and the sign that said *Vacancy* was still beckoning to travelers who needed a place to sleep. John Hayden was never quite sure why he decided to park beyond the entrance, but something prompted him to let the car roll past, and he finally came to a stop under an ancient and towering elm tree that cast black shadows upon the street.

When he had turned off his lights and cut the motor, he walked back, keeping to the same side of the street and seeing again the cars that had been parked in the quadrangle. In contrast to the lighted windows which were shaded by drawn Venetian blinds, the parking area had a darkened and deserted look, but the office glowed brightly and he thought he saw someone at the desk through a crack in the shade as he started across the street toward the tavern.

Jerry was still presiding and several of the regulars were perched on stools watching something on the television set, which was placed high in one corner of the room. Later he was to remember that he did not see Doris Lamar, but at the moment he paid no attention to anything at all in the room except the empty space at the near end of the bar. Although Hayden seldom came there in the evening, Jerry's broad muscular face showed no surprise at seeing him and he made no comment when Hayden asked for a double brandy, with water on the side.

"How much, Jerry?" he asked when the drink was served.

"That will be a dollar and a half, Mr. Hayden."

Hayden counted out the money and Jerry went away. He studied the small snifter glass, which was now nearly full. He stood that way for a while, unmindful of those about him or the dialogue from the television set, recalling again Roger Denham's advice and concentrating on keeping a tight grip on his emotions. He was not, as Denham had told Marion, an aggressive man by nature; yet he knew he was going to have trouble keeping his hands in his pockets, as Denham had advised. Without ever having met Adler, he already hated the man and he knew that to talk sensibly and with calculation in his present condition would be difficult.

That was why he needed the brandy. That was why he did not savor its bouquet and enjoy it as a connoisseur would. He sipped and sipped again. He took a swallow of water. He got a cigarette going. He held out one hand, palm down, as he had done in his kitchen earlier and was pleased to see that the extended fingers were steady. Then, the impatience beginning to ride him, he swallowed the last of the brandy, followed it with a gulp of water, and walked out into the night.

The wide main street was empty as he crossed it. After the friendly warmth of the tavern the night seemed raw, the wind coming in gusts that swayed the glowing motel sign and brought forth protesting metallic sounds. Sedans and station wagons gleamed darkly in the reflected light from the occupied units and, recalling that Doris Lamar had said Sam Adler had room twelve, he angled past the office and started down the center of the quadrangle. It was then that he saw the woman.

At no time did he get a good look at her. He saw her but vaguely as she moved on the cement walk that connected the units in the left-hand building, but she vanished almost instantly and he thought she had come out to get something from one of the cars. He slowed his steps slightly because he did not want to frighten her. He stopped a moment to peer ahead of him and when he did not see her again he wondered where she had gone.

The motel had been built in two facing and parallel sections, and the parking area was partly open at the far end. Between the end units was space for two cars and beyond this was a scraggly hedge which separated the property from the vacant lot facing the next street. There was only one car here now, and although he had heard nothing to indicate that a car door had been opened or closed, he realized the wind might have muffled the sound. He also knew that what the woman did—if in fact it was a woman—was none of his business. His business was with Sam Adler and he cut between two parked cars, angling to the connecting sidewalk so he could examine the unit numbers. By then he knew that Sam Adler had the last room on the right, the one with the car parked beside it, a small, new-looking sedan with New York license plates.

The blinds had been slanted in the room beyond to give it privacy, but lights were on and he found satisfaction in the knowledge that Adler was home. Somewhere inside, a radio was playing softly and he knocked confidently, then knocked again.

He turned as he waited, wondering if the woman he thought he had seen was watching him. When there was no acknowledgment beyond the door, his impatience prompted him to knock once more before he tried the knob.

When it turned easily he pushed into the lighted room saying: "Adler?" as he stopped and swung the door behind him. For another moment he thought the room was empty but a door, apparently giving on the lighted bathroom, was partly closed and he called again: "Hey, Adler!"

There was still no answer and, not understanding why this should be, he took another step, his troubled eyes busy, a sudden tension winding his nerves as instinct telegraphed its first sharp warning. It was this extra movement that brought a new angle of vision and finally told him that he was not alone.

A low chest obscured part of the still figure that was sprawled beyond it, but he could see the hips, the legs, the oddly twisted shoes which lay close together and parallel with the floor.

Unable yet to understand what had happened but certain now that something was horribly wrong, he called again, not knowing that he did so. Some inner compulsion that was both automatic and irresistible made him move again and then he saw it all, the dark-stained white shirt, the slanted neck with the face turned toward the wall, the widespread arms with the limp-fingered hands that curled inward.

He stood very still then, a cold and frightening emptiness inside him as he stared down at this man he had never seen before, and even then, as his mind struggled for some answer, he seemed to know that Sam Adler must be dead.

CHAPTER 5

JOHN HAYDEN WAS NOT aware of time as he stood tense and immobile, breath held and his heart beginning to pound. The recorded playing of some dance band came softly from the radio in a syncopated beat, and with his feet still anchored by the shock of his discovery, he swiveled his head and glanced slowly about the room.

It was, he saw at once, the sort of unit known as an efficiency. Without actually tabulating its contents, he was aware that the furniture was constructed of some blond wood and in a style that was more modern than traditional. The two beds, which were placed at right angles along two walls, had slipcovers and pillows to make them look like couches until they were ready for use. Opposite the partly opened bathroom door was a cubicle with a built-in dresser and some coat hangers on a metal rod, and the end of the room directly ahead of him contained a shallow kitchenette. Here there were cabinets and cupboards, a sink, a counter, an enameled unit that contained a small icebox and an even smaller electric range on top. From where he stood he could see two glasses and a bottle of gin, nearly empty now, bottles of soda, the pulpy halves of lemons from which the juice had been squeezed.

His unconscious inspection completed, he brought his glance back to the man on the floor and now he moved reluctantly toward him. The torso had been turned so that it rested partly on one side, and as he leaned down he saw the reason for the wide, dark stain that glistened moistly on the white shirt.

Because Adler's back was away from him and not far from the wall it lay partly in shadow but he could see the wooden knife handle protruding from the ribs just to the left of the spine. The shape of that handle suggested that it was a kitchen knife and he thought it had probably come from the unit at the end of the room.

He remembered the description that had been given him by Doris Lamar and knew it fitted the sharp-featured face that now looked slack and gray and lifeless. The sleek, black hair needed cutting. There was a dark smudge of beard along the angle of one jaw and the nose, in profile, had a broad and flattened look. The hand that he finally reached for seemed surprisingly warm and limp, and he tried to concentrate now as he sought a pulse beat that never came.

He straightened slowly then, traces of shock still mingling with the confusion in his mind. He could feel the dampness in his palms and his breath came shallowly as he tried to put his thoughts in order. It took a while to relate Adler's death to his own problems, and his first reaction was one of relief as he understood that the man no longer posed a threat to his happiness. The thought shamed him even as it came to him, but it did not last long. For he remembered other details now, and that fleeting sense of relief gave way at once to a fear that was real, genuine, and greatly disturbing.

This fear did not spring from any thought that he would be suspected or charged with murder, and he wasted no time speculating on the reason for Sam Adler's death. The fear he felt came from remembered details that Marion had told him earlier. Adler had shown her a photograph of her first husband; he had shown her a second photograph of fingerprints that he insisted belonged to Ted Corbin. Therefore these photographs had to be on the body or somewhere in this room.

Under other circumstances there would have been no hesitation on Hayden's part. His life had been well ordered and he had an inbred respect for the law that came from a proper background. The thing to do was to call the police immediately and let them take it from there. This was what the sensible part of his mind told him, but the things that had happened to him in the past two or three hours had shaken him mentally, morally, and emotionally.

Nothing that had happened to him before had equipped him to handle such a situation, but he was certain that the first thing the police would do would be to search the room. When they found those photographs they would eventually uncover the very things that he had been trying to protect. By digging into the past they would eventually know why Sam Adler had come here and what he had been trying to do. All this added up to a fine motive for murder, and the thought of what could happen induced a sense of panic that could have distorted his thinking.

Still undecided and torn between two conflicting demands, he backed away and made a slow, deliberate tour of the room. He moved to the kitchenette and saw again the gin and the bottles and glasses and the squeezed lemons. He continued on to the lighted bathroom and pushed the door open with his elbow. As he stepped inside he was at once aware of the distinctive odor that lingered in the air. It was a perfumed smell, not strong but definite; it also had a quality that he did not think had come from the plastic bottle of after-shave lotion which stood beside the razor and toilet kit on the glass shelf above the bowl. This was a more perfumed smell, more feminine, and as he backed from the room he remembered again the woman he had thought he had seen in the darkness of the quadrangle.

The thought did not linger because by now he knew what had to be done. In the light of what happened later, there were times when he doubted the wisdom of his decision, but he did not stop to consider whether he was acting wisely; he was motivated by those inner fears and emotions that revolved about himself and Marion and the threat Sam Adler had made to their future together.

Adler had shown Marion two photographs. They must therefore be somewhere in the room now. Without them the police could find no link between Adler and the past. A likely place to keep them would be a man's wallet, and while he shrank from any contact with the lifeless figure he started toward it, only to stop when he saw the sport coat draped over the back of a chair.

He tried the outside pockets first but found only a pack of cigarettes and paper matches and two sticks of gum. But the inner pockets revealed a coat-type wallet of worn pigskin and he quickly found the two glossy prints in the center fold. He saw that they were about three inches by four, one showing the prints of four fingers of a right hand, the other a well-focused snapshot of a bareheaded man in coveralls. He took a moment to study this one and realize that his wife's impression had been correct. The background did indeed suggest a filling station and there was some insignia on the breast pocket of the coveralls the man wore.

When he had first begun to call on Marion there had been a cabinet photograph of her first husband in her apartment. This had disappeared after their engagement, but he was as convinced now as she had been that this was an unposed snapshot of Ted Corbin. That he seemed older-looking and leaner than the remembered man in the other photograph seemed to bear out Adler's contention that the picture had been taken recently.

A quick inspection of the inner pocket of the wallet revealed no other pictures, but he did find a Social Security card and two driver's licenses. One had been issued in New York State and gave a Flushing address. When he saw that this was an old license he turned to the other, which gave a Conti Street address in Mobile, Alabama. He copied this address in a small notebook before he replaced the wallet, and now a new and urgent thought came to him that was at once discouraging.

If there were photographic prints there had to be negatives. If these were found they would be equally damaging. With this thought in mind he began a quick but thorough search of the room. He made himself bend over the body and pat the hip pockets. He searched the suitcase and the small blue flight bag. He went through the pockets of the gray suit that hung in the alcove and did the same thing to the blue topcoat. The drawers in the chest and the built-in vanity held nothing to interest him, and when he finally ran out of places to look, he was forced to accept the fact that there were no negatives in the room.

But if there were prints there *had* to be negatives. So where were they?

He repeated the question aloud, a sense of frustration growing in him until he realized that time could be important and he was wasting it. He did not think he had been here long, and as he stepped to the door he told himself that no one could prove he had been here tonight. Or could they?

"How about fingerprints?" he said, half aloud.

What had he touched that might betray him? Not the bathroom door because he had opened that with his elbow. The drawer pulls? No, they were too small. The wallet was something else again and he removed it, rubbed it with his handkerchief, and replaced it gingerly. That left only the outer doorknob, and as he reached for it, handkerchief in hand, one more thought came to nag him.

Marion knew he was coming here but he felt certain he could trust her to say the right thing. But how about Roger Denham? Denham knew he was coming. If questioned, Denham would naturally say so. True, Denham could be cautioned not to give the facts as he knew them, but that might imply guilt and he did not want to be under that sort of obligation to the lawyer. Then, even as he considered the problem, a solution came to him.

The door had been unlocked when he came. All he had to do now was to release the safety catch, thereby locking it. Whoever discovered the body would have to admit that the door was locked from outside and this was exactly what he would tell the police if they ever questioned him.

"I'll admit I came to see Adler," he'd say to them. "I knocked and no one answered. I tried the door. It was locked. I figured he was out. There was no way of knowing when he'd be back, so I went home."

Still with the handkerchief in his hand, he inched the door open, fixed the lock, and mentally crossed his fingers as he prepared to leave. If someone saw him now it would be too bad, but it was a chance he had to take, so he sucked in his breath and went out quickly, closing the door behind him.

The darkness seemed complete after the lighted room but he stepped close to the side of the car with the New York license plates and stood in a half-crouch until his eyes adjusted themselves. He could see nothing, hear nothing but the muted sounds of the radio. Because he did not dare walk the length of the quadrangle and expose himself to the lights of the office and the motel sign, he moved the other way, peering for an opening in the hedge at the rear and finding one, then circling around the far side of the building until he reached the elm, which cast its inky shadow over his car.

He coasted into his garage a few minutes later and came to a stop beside the station wagon. He turned out his headlights and stepped to the floor and then he had to grope in the darkness for the switch that activated the overhead bulb. In doing so he stumbled, and as he put out a hand to steady himself his fingers found the hood of the station wagon. It was then that he became aware of the warmth of the metal and, not quite believing his senses or understanding how this could be, he moved forward, his hand finding the ornamental grille in front of the radiator.

By then he was sure. There could be no mistaking the heat in the radiator and he stayed where he was as his mind raced on, disturbed and strangely frightened by his discovery and the knowledge that Marion had used the car, and recently.

But how recently? And for what purpose?

He tried to tell himself that this was not unusual, that there was some simple and innocent explanation. A trip to the drugstore for a prescription or some toiletry or a late newspaper. This, he knew, had happened before, but even as he acknowledged the possibility he remembered again the woman he had seen so briefly at the motel, the distinctive odor of perfume in the lighted bathroom. To arrest such unwanted imagery he glanced at his watch and was surprised to see that it was still only ten minutes after nine.

This, he told himself as he pulled down the overhead door and turned toward the breezeway, was all to the good, and as he crossed the area to the darkened kitchen he outlined the tentative timetable which began with his prompt arrival at Roger Denham's place at eight o'clock.

He had been there no more than a half hour, if that. Another ten minutes, say eight-forty, had brought him to Jerry's Tavern. Five minutes with his brandy would put him at Sam Adler's door at eight-forty-five or a minute later. Since it was about a ten-minute drive from the tavern here, he must have been at the motel no more than twelve or fourteen minutes.

And he not only had the two pictures; he had not been seen. So what should he do about Marion? Ask her where she'd been or pretend he did not know she had been gone? This, he knew at once, would be best, and he was determined to stick with the decision as he entered the kitchen and locked the door behind him.

CHAPTER 6

He did not stop in the kitchen but continued on into the lighted living room, expecting to find his wife in her chair and wondering just what he was going to say to her. Then, even as he brought some discipline to his thoughts, he realized that the effort was wasted. The room was empty and the only light came from a floor lamp by the wing chair.

For a second or two as he stood there he felt a welcome sense of relief, but it did not last when he remembered the station wagon and its warm radiator. Because he knew she must be home he moved quietly to the inner hall. From there he could see the open door of their bedroom and the darkness beyond. Still moving soundlessly, he reached the doorway and peered inside. There was enough light behind him to reveal the elongated mound her body made under the covers and the dark hair spread upon the pillow.

The fact that she had gone to bed early was, in itself, not unusual. In the last couple of months there had been several times when she had retired soon after dinner and he understood the reason for this. On those occasions he would come into their darkened room and undress as quietly as he could. Sometimes she would be awake, or would waken, and he would slip into bed beside her and hold her until she fell asleep again. At other times, knowing that she was asleep and not wanting to disturb her, he would move down the hall to the guest bedroom. The fact that the light was already on here was her way of telling him that tonight she was inviting him to sleep alone, and he stood another moment, watching for some sign of movement and wondering whether she was asleep or whether she was afraid of the questions he might ask.

The thought brought with it a sense of frustration but it gave him little alternative and he went back to the kitchen and turned on the light. The dishes they had used for their soup and salad earlier had been rinsed and stacked on the counter and he now put them into the dishwasher. He thought about making a drink and knew he did not want one. But he wanted something and he compromised by getting a beer from the refrigerator. He took this into the living room, and when he had a cigarette going he eased into the chair, his somber gaze fixed but unseeing and his mouth set grimly as his mind began again to grapple with his problems.

He made no conscious effort to think; he simply could not help himself. He found himself wondering how long it would be before Sam Adler's body was discovered. He wondered what course the police investigation would take, and as he recalled again the story of George Freeman's fight with the stranger he found a new motive for Adler's death. Freeman was the quiet type that no one seemed to know too well. That he was intensely jealous where Doris Lamar was concerned seemed obvious in the light of what had happened, but he realized now that there was no point in trying to imagine what Freeman might do under extreme provocation.

Once the investigation was under way, the police would be sure to learn about the relationship between Freeman and Doris Lamar and Sam Adler. But—and this thought jarred him—they might also learn from Doris that Adler had been asking questions about him. Suppose they came here to ask other questions. Suppose someone had seen Marion tonight when she was out in the station wagon. Suppose...

This line of reasoning angered him and he swore aloud. Such disloyalty shamed him and he told himself again that Marion could not have killed Adler; she could not kill anyone. She was a completely normal, well-adjusted, and sensible girl. She always had been. The fact that her pregnancy had given her some moments of emotional turbulence could not possibly have brought her to the point of violence. This is what he told himself and this is what he believed, and yet some obscure segment of his brain that he could not control persisted in asserting itself.

He could not forget the knife that had been thrust into Sam Adler's back. It was, he felt sure, a kitchen knife of some sort, and the obvious assumption was that it had come from the kitchenette in Adler's room. But he could not dismiss the thought that Adler had been stabbed in the back. It was hard for him to understand why a man would use this method unless the killing was premeditated. But to a woman a kitchen knife was a familiar object. Driven by fear or desperation or a moment of temporary insanity, a woman wanting to strike back and finding such a knife handy might use it.

He lost track of time as he sat there brooding, his beer forgotten and growing flat in the glass. In an effort to curb his imagination and to submerge his present doubts and fears, he forced his mind back into the past while he considered the girl he had married, not just as he knew her since they had been together, but before that, before Ted Corbin.

She had been brought up in Westchester in a family that was socially acceptable and soundly rooted. As Marion Haskell there was enough money for a good finishing school and a college education, even though the Haskells had never been wealthy. Her father worked in Wall Street and his speculations were not always too wise, so that when a heart attack took him a month or so before Marion was to graduate from Vassar, there was not a great deal left except the house, two small insurance policies payable to her and her brother, and a large one that went to her mother, who, for the past few years, had been living with her son in Texas.

Marion had gone to work for an advertising agency in New York immediately after graduation. She had been sharing an apartment with another girl when she met Ted Corbin, who was a friend of a friend of her roommate's. Corbin was working as a paper salesman at the time, and the factors that caused the marriage to founder after three years were the very ones that attracted Marion to him in the first place.

That Corbin was a big, good-looking, and easygoing man was at once in his favor, but what intrigued her most was the fact that he was so different from the young men she had gone out with in the past. Mostly these were Ivy League youths whose standards, conduct, and ambitions were so similar to her own. The pattern was familiar to her and she enjoyed being with them; the affairs that she had with one or another from time to time were in a minor key, but always the language they shared was the same.

Since Ted Corbin had not been trained to fit the pattern, he presented an approach that Marion found both different and exciting. For Corbin had been born and brought up in a small Pennsylvania mining town, and if his intelligence quotient was perhaps less than some, he had other skills, one of which was the ability to play a hard and aggressive type of football that was much in demand. This got him into a school in South Carolina, and by the time he had graduated he had gained some prominence in his field. He had lasted two years in the professional league, and when he realized he would never be a first-string regular, he had taken a job with a southern paper company, which eventually brought him to New York.

The fact that he was not adept or skilled in social intercourse did not seem important to Marion, even though she was aware of this. She liked his breeziness, his easy manners, his offhand ways; it was only much later that she discovered these ways were a little crude, a little too coarse for her taste. For he was, basically, an outdoor man. He liked to hunt and fish and go to the fights or the ball game. He had not read a book since he left college and she discovered that he had no intention of ever reading another. His taste in newspapers was limited to the tabloids or the sporting pages. His friends were not her friends, and even though he tried at times, the lack of communication eventually made him sullen and distant.

Friction developed early in the marriage but they tried in their own ways to combat it. But it was harder for Corbin because there was little depth to his thinking and he did not have the basic equipment to adjust to new things. Discouraged by his failure to make the marriage go, he had sought comfort in earlier friends. He drank too much and had difficulty in holding a job. There had been three jobs in three years, and he was on his way to see about a fourth when tragedy struck the aircraft. Even before that, they both knew that their marriage was finished. They had practically agreed on a separation and Marion had started to look for another job in the advertising field....

The sound that cut through Hayden's thoughts and made him jump in the chair so startled him that for the moment he did not know whether it came from the telephone or the front door. It took him another few seconds to break the spell of nervous tension that gripped him, to glance at his watch, to understand that he had been sitting here for nearly two hours. For it was now a few minutes after eleven, and as the sound was repeated and he came to his feet, he understood that whoever had rung the doorbell had not come here on a social call. He moved quickly then, the trepidation growing in him as his pulse quickened.

He did not know the two men who faced him as he opened the door, but he saw that one was tall and lean-looking in his trench coat, the other somewhat shorter and more heavily built. It was the tall one who made the introduction.

"Mr. Hayden?"

"That's right."

"I'm Lieutenant Garvey of the State Police.... This is County Detective Ball from the State's Attorney's office."

Hayden's acknowledgment was a mumbled "Hello," and although he had already considered the possibility of such a call, he was glad the light was at his back. For in those first moments he could feel his features stiffen as the blood drained from his face. He had the impression that the shadowed eyes beneath the hat brims were intent upon his reactions and he concentrated on making his voice sound reasonably surprised but not disconcerted.

"What can I do for you?"

"We're sorry to bother you at this hour," Garvey said, "but we need some information and we thought you might help us. May we come in?"

"Certainly." Hayden stepped back and waved them toward the living room. "In there. Take off your coats."

They removed their hats and unbuttoned their coats but did not take them off. They sat down on the divan and he could see now that Garvey was in his late thirties, a confident-looking man with a prominent jaw, deep-set gray eyes, and short brown hair. Ball was older and more round in the face. His head was nearly bald on top and Hayden was at once aware of the dark eyes which were steady, watchful, and inquisitive.

"I was just having a beer before I went to bed," he said, and took a swallow of the stale brew to prove it. "Can I offer you anything?"

"No thanks," they said.

"We'll try not to keep you up," Garvey said. "But we'd like to find out what you know about a man named Adler."

CHAPTER 7

JOHN HAYDEN TOOK ANOTHER slow and deliberate swallow of the beer and reached for a cigarette. He knew then that he was as ready as he ever would be for the questions and it pleased him to see that the flame from their table lighter was steady when he held it up. He could still feel his pulse but it was no longer racing, and he frowned deliberately at the end of the cigarette before he replied.

"Adler?" he said on a note of puzzlement.

"You don't know him?" Ball asked.

"I don't think so. At least I don't remember anyone by that name."

"He was staying at The Shady Maple Motel."

Hayden frowned again for their benefit. "What about him? Is he in some kind of trouble?"

"Not any more."

"Someone stuck a knife in his back," Garvey said. "According to the medical examiner he probably died somewhere between eight and nine o'clock tonight."

Hayden heard them out and then, nothing showing in his face, he rose and moved over to close the door to the inner hall.

"My wife went to bed early," he said. "She's four months pregnant and I'd like her to get her rest." He came back and sat down. He looked right at them. "I don't know anyone named Adler," he said, "but I'm curious to know why you came here at all."

"We've been making a lot of inquiries, Mr. Hayden," Ball said. "From things we've heard we got the impression that you *did* know Adler."

"To the best of my knowledge I never laid eyes on the man."

"George Freeman—he's managing The Shady Maple—" Garvey began.

"I know him."

"—found the body around nine-thirty, or so he says. He couldn't tell us much about Adler except that he was a stranger who registered yesterday afternoon."

"We started to check on him," Ball said. "We put some men on the main street to see what we could find. You know Lee Cramer at the filling station, don't you?"

"Know him well."

"He remembered Adler. He had some conversation with him yesterday afternoon and Adler asked if he knew you. He asked where you lived and Cramer told him. Now why would Adler do that if he didn't intend to get in touch with you?"

"Cramer told me about that conversation," Hayden said and was pleased that his voice sounded so steady and unruffled. "He described the man but he didn't mention any name."

Garvey, who had been examining a small, leather-covered notebook, looked up. "We made some inquiries at Jerry's Tavern," he said. "The way we get it you stopped in there twice tonight."

"That's right."

"You had some conversation with the waitress there—Doris Lamar—"

"That was around a quarter of six."

"Mind telling us the substance of that conversation?"

"It was mostly about her and George Freeman."

"Did she tell you that a man named Sam Adler had been making some inquiries about you?"

Hayden hesitated but not for long.

"Yes, now that I stop to think of it. She said she and George had had an argument about something. Adler made a play for her the night before and she decided to put Freeman in his place. They went dancing later at the Log Cabin and Freeman came in and took a swing at Adler and Adler beat him to the punch. When I saw Freeman he was wearing dark glasses. He looked as if he had a shiner."

"He did," Ball said. "It was a beaut."

"So Adler asked Lee Cramer if he knew you and where you lived," Garvey continued. "Cramer told him. Tonight Doris Lamar told you the same thing. But you still say you don't know Adler?"

"That's right."

"He didn't come here to see you?"

"He did not."

"And you have no idea what he wanted?"

"No."

"Where were you this evening?" Ball asked.

Hayden suddenly found it difficult to meet the unremitting steadiness of the county detective's dark gaze. The uneasiness was growing in him now and for some reason his thoughts moved off on a tangent and he found himself comparing these two with the detectives he had seen on television and in the movies. He had never been questioned by a policeman about anything, but the detectives he had seen on the screen were hard-nosed, tough-talking characters who threw their weight around and wore down suspects by intimidation and threats. In contrast, these two men spoke quietly and in matter-of-fact tones. They were polite, and at the moment well mannered, but he understood that they would be relentless in their pursuit of any information they thought pertinent.

He thought about the two photographs he had in his pocket and was thankful that they could not know about them. There had been moments of misgivings when he left the motel room, but he was glad now that he had acted the way he did. They might pin him down on this or that, but without those pictures which linked him and Marion with the past there was no motive—unless they somehow located the original negatives.

"I had an appointment with my attorney at eight o'clock."

"Who would that be?" Garvey asked.

"Roger Denham," Hayden said and mentioned the address.

"You went to his house?"

"That's right."

"When did you leave?"

"I'd say around eight-thirty."

"Then what?"

"I stopped at Jerry's Tavern."

"For a drink?" Ball asked in his customary even tones.

"Naturally."

"What did you order?"

"A double brandy and water," Hayden said, and even as he spoke he knew that the announcement would bring forth additional comment.

"Was that the usual thing for you at that time of the evening?" Garvey asked.

"No. I felt like a double brandy and I ordered it. I drank it and drove home."

"Jerry said that when you left you started across the street toward the motel," Ball said.

"Sure," Hayden said, "because my car was parked on that side of the street."

"You got home about when?"

"Nine, or a little after."

Ball leaned back and exchanged glances with the lieutenant. Apparently this was sufficient for a silent meeting of the minds because when he continued he seemed to speak for both of them.

"We'd like very much to speak to your wife for a few minutes, Mr. Hayden,"
he said. "I know it may seem to you like an imposition and I appreciate her
condition, but in a murder case it's important that we find out as much as we
can and as quickly as we can. Perhaps if you explained—"

He did not finish the sentence but stopped abruptly, his gaze shifting and
the dark eyes opening. In the next instant he started to rise and so did Lieutenant Garvey. The reaction was so surprising that Hayden turned; not until
then did he realize that his wife was standing in the doorway, her hand still
on the knob.

"I thought I heard voices," she said. "Is something wrong, darling?"

He got to his feet as she spoke, and even with all the confusion in his mind
he had time to notice how pretty she looked. She had never been a girl who
went to bed with cream on her face or curlers in her hair, except when it had
just been washed; now her face had a clean, scrubbed look, and her dark hair
was caught at the nape with a ribbon. The hazel eyes had a sleepy look and
the dark blue robe she wore was long and tailored. He found his tongue as he
stepped to her side and drew her into the room.

"Marion, this is Lieutenant Garvey and Detective Ball—my wife."

The two men said: "How do you do, Mrs. Hayden," and looked impressed.

"Police officers, darling?" she said with just the right inflection. "But why?"
She smiled at them. "Please sit down. Tell me about it."

"A man named Sam Adler was killed sometime this evening at The Shady
Maple Motel," Hayden said before the two detectives could reply. "Someone
stabbed him. They seem to think we might know him."

He saw the effect of his words on her as she sat down. The long lashes lifted
and her eyes were suddenly wide open and staring at him. He watched the
slackness working on her mouth and the color slowly drain from her face. It
was a frightening thing to see, this change in her face, and he was terribly
afraid that she might blurt out the things she knew before she had a chance
to think. He knew she was about to speak, and he could not stop her, and it
came to him then that the look of shock and fear in her eyes was concerned
not with the two officers but with him.

She knows that I was going to see Adler, he thought. *She's wondering if I killed
him and how can I tell her I didn't?*

"Stabbed?" she said in a tone that matched the look on her face. "How
awful."

She looked at the two men on the divan. She looked back at Hayden. The
paleness was still in her cheeks but her eyes had narrowed slightly and were
no longer unguarded. She frowned, and he knew this was deliberate. He was
grateful for the intelligence and resiliency that enabled her to regain her

composure and her wits so quickly. Her voice sounded just right when she continued.

"But I don't understand," she said. "Surely"—she looked at Garvey and then at Ball—"you don't think we know anything about it."

"We're just checking now, Mrs. Hayden," Ball said. "We know he arrived in town yesterday afternoon and we know he asked some questions about your husband." He went on to repeat the information he had given to Hayden. He took time to let her digest what he had said before he continued. "What about you, Mrs. Hayden?"

"Me?"

"Did you know Adler?" He hesitated and when she did not reply he said: "Doesn't it seem a little odd that this man should come into town and ask where the Haydens live and then not bother to look them up?"

He apparently expected no answer and Garvey took over. "In cases like these we sometimes get a break," he said. "Like tonight for instance. In trying to get a line on Adler and find out what he was doing here we talked to a lot of people. We spent some time at Jerry's Tavern and there was a fellow at the bar who overheard what we were saying to Jerry and the waitress."

"His name is James," Ball said. "He runs a television repair shop and he had to make a call on your road this afternoon. As a matter of fact it was at the Lamsons'." He took time to direct his steady gaze at Marion and then at Hayden.

That gave Hayden time enough to brace himself because he knew what was coming. He did not know the details but he knew that the Lamsons lived no more than sixty or seventy yards down the road and he understood that Ball would not take this line of questioning unless he already knew enough to prove his point, whatever it was. There was nothing to do but sit there and wait for the detective to continue and presently he did.

"This fellow James asked about Adler. He wanted to know what he looked like and what kind of a car he drove. The reason for his curiosity was that when he had finished his service call and was putting the ladder on his truck he noticed this sedan with the New York license plates."

He paused, as though waiting for some reaction before he said: "Before he drove off he noticed this man come out of your house and get into the car. He described the man and the description fitted Adler. We took him over and let him look at the body. He says that's the man he saw this afternoon."

Again Hayden could only wait and hope. Because he was afraid to watch his wife's face he reached for another cigarette and fumbled with the light. He wanted desperately to help her, but as he tried to think of something to say she proved she needed no help.

"Oh—is that the man you're talking about?" she said with just the right emphasis. "Yes. He was here this afternoon."

Garvey said: "Ahh—"

Ball said: "What did he want?"

"He was a book salesman."

The reply seemed to stop them for a second. They took time to peer at her before they exchanged quick glances.

"What kind of books, Mrs. Hayden?" Ball asked.

"Some children's encyclopedia."

"He just happened to stop here?"

"Not exactly. He said a friend—he wouldn't give any name—told him we might be interested in such a set."

"Did he show you the set?"

"He was hardly here long enough for that. I told him we weren't interested."

"That's funny," Garvey said.

"What's funny?" Hayden said, proud of his wife's response and hoping to take the pressure off of her.

"Book salesmen usually carry books," Garvey said. "A lot of them have sample bindings. The idea is that when they hook you for a set they try to sell you the most expensive binding they can. But you didn't see any books, did you?"

"No."

"Or any sample bindings?"

"No."

"There were no books in Adler's room," Ball said, making the sentence sound like an accusation. "No samples of any kind. There were no books and no bindings in his car either.... Maybe he showed you some literature about that set of books," he added, "like some circulars or folders."

Hayden cut in because he could not keep silent any longer. Marion's composure had been steadfast and magnificent, but he could see the strain showing in her face and he was not sure how long she could maintain her self-control in the face of such persistent questioning.

"Look, gentlemen," he said. "It's late. I've told you about my wife's condition. We've tried to co-operate with you—"

"We appreciate that," Ball said.

"A man named Adler was stabbed to death," Hayden continued, his words quick and aggressive now. "You seem to think we know something about it. I've told you I don't know the man. You heard what my wife said. It seems to me you might make more progress concentrating on someone who had a motive for murder."

"If you mean Freeman," Garvey said, "we intend to. But we also have to find out all we can about Adler and the sooner the better."

"Bear with us for another minute or two," Ball said. "A couple of questions and we'll take a recess until tomorrow. We're curious about a phone call Adler made." He paused, as though wanting to be sure they understood him.

"The rooms at The Shady Maple have telephones," he said, "but calls have to be made through the office. At around eight-fifteen a call came from Adler's room. He asked Freeman for a number. Freeman wrote it down and dialed. Now, according to him, he makes a point of never listening in on a conversation once the connection is made, so this time he waited just long enough to hear the number answer before he cut out. This call was completed. A woman answered. We checked the number. It's listed in your name, Mr. Hayden."

He paused again to give Marion his attention and Hayden was afraid to look at her. For it seemed now that this was the answer to the warm radiator on the station wagon. Adler had phoned her and Marion had apparently gone to see him, and now the truth would come out....

"What did he want, Mrs. Hayden?" Ball continued.

"I don't know."

"What?"

"There was no such call."

"But Freeman—"

"I don't know Mr. Freeman, but I'm afraid he was mistaken about this number."

She was looking right at Ball when she answered and her chin was up. At that moment she had command of her emotions and Hayden was both surprised and pleased by her defiance. He also knew that the two officers did not believe her. Their expressions said so. As their glances met, Garvey gave a faint shrug and Ball tried once more.

"You're sure of this?" he asked.

"Quite sure."

They stood up and started to button their coats and Garvey said: "You were here all evening, Mrs. Hayden?"

"That's right."

"What time did your husband leave?"

"Well"—she frowned to show that she was considering the question—"he had an appointment at eight."

"With Mr. Denham?"

She hesitated just long enough to give Hayden a quick glance before she said: "Yes. I suppose it was about ten or twelve minutes of eight when he left."

"And what time did he come back?"

"I'm not quite sure."

"Oh?"

"You see, I haven't been feeling too well. I went to bed shortly after John left."

"You didn't hear him come in then?"

"I sort of heard him. I mean I was about half asleep and half awake when I heard his car come into the garage. I didn't turn on the light then or look at the clock."

She stood as she finished and straightened the robe. She gave them a polite nod and said she hoped they would excuse her. When she turned away, Hayden started for the front door and the two officers followed. As they stepped out into the night they thanked him again for his co-operation. They said they would be in touch with him tomorrow and it was possible that the State's Attorney might want to question him and his wife again.

CHAPTER 8

BY THE TIME JOHN Hayden came back to the living room the hall door was closed and he thought Marion had gone to bed, but when he stepped from the kitchen where he had gone to rinse out the beer glass she was waiting for him. He saw, as he stopped in front of her, that the look of composure and aloofness she had maintained for so long had dissolved into one of concern and helplessness. The hazel eyes seemed close to tears as they searched his face, and reaction made her voice unsteady as she put up her arms and said:

"Hold me. Hold me tight, please."

He drew her swiftly to him, grateful for the chance, his palms hard against the small of her back as her arms encircled his neck. He could feel the softness of her body, the full length of it. He could feel her tremble before she relaxed, and the fragrance of her hair was in the back of his throat as her head snuggled against his jaw. She kept it there and spoke against the side of his neck.

"Remember before you left when I told you not to touch me?"

"Yes."

"I couldn't help it. I love you, darling. I know I'm being unreasonable, but if Ted is alive—oh, I don't know how to explain it—"

"Don't try."

"You do understand?"

He was not sure that he did. He knew that it had something to do with this thought in the back of her mind that questioned the legality of their marriage and robbed them of the right to live as husband and wife. He did not agree but he could not argue the point now, because her closeness and the pressure of her body wakened old desires and brought new tensions. He had to swallow before he could speak but he lied convincingly.

"Sure," he said. "Just don't worry about it. We'll work it out."

The words seemed to comfort her. She uttered a small, muffled sob and caught her breath, and then her arms relaxed and he knew the moment had passed. He let her go and she tried to smile up at him, and he could see the relief in the wet brightness of her eyes.

"All right," she said and took another deep breath. "We've got to talk," she said and backed into a chair. "Did you go to see him, John?"

"Adler? Yes. He was already dead."

"Then the police were trying to trap us."

"Trap us? How do you mean?"

She crossed her knees and seemed unaware that one leg was exposed beneath the dark blue robe. She leaned forward, her look intent.

"But don't you see? Adler had those two pictures with him. The police would search his room and his clothes and his wallet, wouldn't they?"

"Sure but—"

"So they couldn't help but find those pictures. They probably already have them. They're bound to find out what they mean."

"How are they?"

"But I've already told you. Ted worked for the government. His fingerprints are on file. How long do you think it will take the police to find out that the fingerprints on that picture belong to him?"

Hayden made no immediate answer. He simply looked at her, a little amazed that she could be so emotionally feminine one moment and so practical the next. There was nothing weak and helpless in her attitude now, and it came to him that the only way he could reassure her was to tell her the truth. Reluctantly then, not sure he was doing the right thing, he took the two photographs from his pocket and displayed them.

"Oh," she said and caught her breath as her eyes snapped open. "You took them."

"I had to, didn't I?"

"But he was dead."

"Certainly he was dead. I walked in and found him and I wanted to get out in a hurry and then I remembered these and knew I had to look. I found them in his wallet."

"Did—did anyone see you?"

"I don't think so."

He slipped the pictures back into his pocket and hoped what he said was true. For he remembered again the woman he had seen so vaguely in the motel quadrangle. She could have seen him, as he saw her. He did not know if she would remember or whether she would be able to describe him. In all that darkness it was even possible that she had not seen him at all. Then, as his mind went on, he knew that there was something else he had to know. He felt certain that she had lied to the two police officers, but it seemed now that it was important to understand to what extent she had lied.

"What about the phone call?" he asked.

"Phone call?"

"Adler did call, didn't he?"

The lashes dipped to obscure her eyes as she hesitated. She seemed to notice the exposed leg and took time to cover it.

"Yes," she said finally, and then her head came up and once more she met his gaze head-on. "But they can't prove it. How can they? This man Freeman can say he dialed this number and I can say he didn't, or at least that I didn't hear it. It's just his word against mine."

This, he knew, was true but it was not enough for him, not now. Quietly, and with no overtones of censure in his voice, he said: "What did he want, baby?"

The unsettling effect of his question was at once apparent. Again she lowered her glance. She picked a piece of lint off the robe and smoothed out the fabric with her fingertips.

"It's sort of hard to explain," she said finally.

"Why?"

"Because I'm not sure I can make you understand."

"Try."

"Well, he was one of those men that seemed to think that all he had to do was make a pass at a woman and she would fall into his arms. I told you what he looked like. He was not bad-looking, actually. You could tell he thought he was pretty smooth. He was very glib and self-assured and much too familiar. At least he tried to be."

"This was this afternoon?"

"Yes. Even when he was telling me what he wanted, when he knew how upset I must be by what he said, he was a little suggestive. He went out of his way to let me know he thought I was something special and men like that are usually hard to discourage."

She lifted one shoulder in an empty shrug and said: "He called me a few minutes after you had left. He said he wanted to see me. I told him he must be out of his mind. I said you would probably stop and see him later but he said that didn't matter. He said there was no reason why I couldn't stop by for a friendly drink. He said he didn't want to be unreasonable and it would be easier if we could talk things over in a friendly way."

"What did you say?"

"I hung up on him."

She paused, watching him now to see if he believed her, and this time he was the one who had to avert his glance. It was a convincing performance, and if he had not been aware of certain facts he might have believed her. As it was, his heart sank and a feeling of hopelessness began to undermine his thoughts. He knew now that she was lying, but some inner impulse he did not understand prevented him from saying so. He dared not accuse her now. He could not tell her that he had felt the radiator of the station wagon.

He believed that Adler had made that call. He believed that she had answered it. The station wagon had been used between the time he left and returned. If she had not gone to see Adler, then where had she gone? If the trip had been an innocent one, why had she not admitted it?

There had been a woman in the darkened quadrangle and that woman could have come from Adler's room. The smell of perfume in the bathroom testified to the fact that a woman had been there for a minute or two and possibly longer. Furthermore Adler had been stabbed in the back by a kitchen knife, a woman's weapon if there ever was one. The combination of such thoughts was so unacceptable that he tried to dismiss them by telling himself that even if Marion had gone to see Adler for some reason he could not understand, she never would have turned to murder. She could have been worked up to the point of desperation and probably was; she never would have gone there otherwise. Her condition had brought occasional moments of emotional instability, but murder was something else. He shook his head to dispel such thoughts, not knowing that he did so. Apparently she saw the movement.

"What's the matter?" she asked anxiously. "Don't you believe me?"

"Certainly I believe you," he said, an edge in his voice he had not intended.

"The way you acted I wasn't so sure."

"And do you believe me?"

"If you mean that he was dead when you found him, of course I do." She frowned then as a new thought came to disturb her. "Do you think Roger will tell them?"

The digression confused him momentarily and he had to concentrate to remember his call on the lawyer and what he had said. Denham, alone, knew that he intended to have it out with Sam Adler, and if the police questioned him, and they probably would since he had already told them of his appointment—The conclusion that came to him served only to add to his uncertainty and discouragement, but he answered as truthfully as he could.

"Probably."

"Perhaps if we asked him—"

"No." Hayden shook his head. "We're not going to ask Denham to lie for me. Being the kind of proper guy he is, I'm not sure he would anyway."

"That's not fair."

"Okay, I'm unfair." He stood up. "But I'm not going to worry about that now. If I have to admit that I went to the motel I will, but no one can prove I actually went into the room. Let's leave it at that for tonight, hunh? Let's cross that bridge when we get to it. Will you do something for me?"

She gave him a quick, suspicious glance before she said: "What?"

"Take a sleeping pill and get some rest. We both need it. Would you like something first? Shall I make some coffee?"

"It would only keep me awake."

"How about some orange juice or a glass of milk?"

"All right." She came slowly to her feet, a sag in her shoulders now and defeat written in the soft lines of her face. "Milk, I guess."

"And a cooky?"

"No cooky."

"I'll bring it in to you," he said and turned away.

In the kitchen he poured two glasses of milk and found a couple of cookies for himself. He took his time and made sure the kitchen was in order. He tried the back door again and then went into the living room to turn off the lights. She was in bed when he entered the room, the covers well up under her chin. He put her glass of milk on the bedside table and looked down at her, trying not to let the worry he felt show in his face.

He went over to the closet and got his pajamas and robe and slippers. He piled them on his arm and put a clean shirt on top of them. Then, not caring what she thought about the legality of their marriage, he went to her and stooped down. He saw again the torment in her eyes before she made that slight turn of her head. He brushed the soft cool cheek with his lips, and as he straightened she reached out and caught his arm. She gave it a hard spasmodic squeeze and then turned quickly on her side, her back toward him.

CHAPTER 9

WEDNESDAY WAS A LONG hard day for John Hayden. The March weather continued raw and windy, and the sky, which was overcast and unpromising when he went to work, remained that way. He got his own breakfast as he did on those mornings when Marion did not feel well, leaving the percolator attached, so that the coffee would be hot when she wanted it. The bedroom door had remained closed as he had left it the night before, and because the thoughts he had taken to bed still remained insidiously in his mind he was glad he did not have to face her so early in the morning.

He made his usual telephone call around noon, but the conversation was polite, stilted, and conventional. There was no reference to their problems and he told her he would be home early. Two conferences with out-of-town clients helped divert his thoughts, but he could not concentrate on the routine of the business day. This was partly due to telephone calls that never came. Each time his buzzer sounded and his secretary spoke he expected some word from the police or the State's Attorney or Roger Denham. As the day dragged on, he felt a mounting irritation that was directed not only at his own dilemma but at those who ignored him.

But he did some constructive thinking and it had as its focus George Freeman and Doris Lamar. For it occurred to him with increasing frequency that little had been said the night before about Freeman by Lieutenant Garvey and Detective Ball.

Last night when he had discovered the body there had been no thought in his mind as to who might have done the killing. He had been too concerned about his personal problems and the two pictures which had become instruments of blackmail. He had made a decision then—to take them and get out. He had taken the gamble and was aware of the risks, but he had been prodded as much by the impulse and perhaps a touch of panic as he had been by a sensible evaluation of the odds.

He had not known then that the station wagon had been used in his absence. The telephone call the officers had mentioned both surprised and shocked him, and although he had always trusted his wife he knew now that she had lied to him.

But what about Freeman? Freeman was in love and he had already demonstrated his jealousy and his hate for Sam Adler the previous evening. Freeman had been brooding when he had seen him in the tavern in the late afternoon. Such jealousy and resentment could have exploded into violence and murder, not premeditated perhaps, but murder nonetheless. From his point of vantage in the motel Freeman could keep track of Adler. So where was he between eight and nine o'clock? If he had an alibi none had been mentioned. And Doris Lamar?

He remembered that he had not seen her when he had ordered the double brandy to steady his nerves. She might, he knew, have been in the kitchen during those brief minutes. But if not, where exactly was she and what had she been doing? Suppose she had sneaked over to the motel to see Adler, and Freeman had known this? There had been this momentary glimpse of some woman in the darkened courtyard. Until now he had considered her shadowy presence something of a possible threat to him, but he understood that it might be the other way round.

Such thoughts continued to plague him as the afternoon wore on, and by four o'clock he knew what he wanted to do. In his present frame of mind he was of no use to the company, and it seemed imperative that he talk to the woman and find out where she had been and how much she knew. It did not occur to him just how he could accomplish all this, but he was aware that she did not go to work until five. When he realized he had time to catch her at her cottage he made up his mind.

He had been there but once, on that rainy night when he offered her a ride, but he had seen the place before, a small three-room-and-bath cottage which stood back of a large, ornate, and run-down mansion that had long been for sale. It had been unoccupied for many months and he saw the signs of decay as he rolled along the driveway and took the fork at the end. He parked under the trees and saw the light in the cottage living room as he climbed two wooden steps to the tiny porch.

There may have been a moment as she opened the door when Doris Lamar's green eyes showed surprise, but experience with men had taught her many things and the reaction was swiftly controlled. She was wearing a figured kimono and her face had a naked look without its make-up. But if she was disconcerted it did not show and her voice was casual and matter-of-fact.

"Oh, hello, Mr. Hayden."

"Hello, Doris," he said. "I'd like to talk to you for a few minutes."

"Well"—she hesitated, pursed her lips, and shrugged indifferently—"I was getting dressed. I have to be at work at five."

"It's important, Doris. It shouldn't take too long."

"All right." She turned away and let him enter and close the door. "I can finish my fingernails while you're talking. Take off your coat if you want to. Throw it over there on the couch."

He slipped off his coat, put it on the couch, and placed his hat on top of it. When he sat down the springs sagged protestingly under his weight and a glance about the squarish room told him that Doris had probably rented it as it stood.

The furniture had neither style nor quality. The carpet had been worn down to the nap in places, the occasional tables needed refinishing, and the slipcovers on two of the chairs were threadbare at the arms; a third chair was a wicker affair with a padded seat. From where he sat he could look into the bedroom and he could also see a corner of the kitchen with its old-fashioned sink and a stove that stood high on spindly metal legs.

The light that he had seen from outside came from a wooden floor lamp with a parchment shade. A circular shelf, which clung to the pedestal like a doughnut, served as a table of sorts and on it was a bottle of nail-polish remover, some cotton, tissues, and a bottle of dark red polish. Doris had pulled her chair close and her head was bent now as she daintily decorated the nails of her left hand.

"When you knocked," she said, "I was afraid it would be another cop or a reporter."

"Did the police question you?"

"Hah!" she said. "For three hours last night. Then they practically got me out of bed this morning and we had another two-hour session."

"Have you seen George Freeman?"

"They were bringing him into Lieutenant Garvey's office at the State Police barracks when I left this morning."

"You haven't seen him since?"

"No."

"What about last night?"

"I saw him when you did. When he had those dark glasses on and was sulking at the bar."

"You didn't see him after he left?"

"No ... Is that what you wanted to talk about?"

"That's part of it, Doris. Freeman was in love with you, wasn't he?"

"I guess he thought he was."

"I understand that jealousy makes a good motive for murder. If he thought Adler was cutting him out"—he hesitated and decided to guess—"if he thought you were going away with him, for instance, he could have gone to Adler's room and—"

"I doubt it," she said flatly. "I doubt if George would have guts enough to kill anyone."

"How much guts does it take to stab a man in the back?"

She considered the question before she said: "I see what you mean. But I don't believe it."

Hayden rose and reached for a cigarette. He went over to offer the woman one and waited while she put the little brush back into the nail-polish bottle. She blew on the fingers of the hand she had just painted and took the cigarette with the other. When she leaned forward to accept a light he could see the dark roots in the blond hair. The front of the kimono had opened slightly and he saw that she had a slip on underneath but no stockings.

"It's Adler that worries me," he said and decided to demonstrate what he meant. He had no intention of telling her the truth but he needed all the help he could get and he was prepared to confide in her up to a point in order to see what sort of reaction he could get. "The police came to see us last night too."

"You mean you and your wife? But why?"

"I thought you might know. Adler came into town a couple of days ago and asked a lot of questions about me. The police found it out and they wanted to know why he was so interested. I told them I never saw the man but I can't seem to get the idea across."

He had been moving idly about the room as he spoke, and now, stopping at the bedroom door, he glanced in and saw the two suitcases which stood against the wall beyond the double bed. For some reason they seemed strangely out of place, and because he found himself wondering if they had any particular significance he spoke of them now.

"Were you going somewhere, Doris?"

He was aware that she was looking at him. And she must have known what had prompted the question because there was no suggestion of reluctance in her reply.

"I may have been."

"With Adler?"

"Does it make any difference?" she said, still watching him. "I'm not going now and that's for sure."

He came back and sat down on the couch. The green eyes were regarding him openly, but he could not tell whether the small gleam he saw in them came from speculation or amusement.

"Are you surprised?" she said. "I mean that Sam Adler could make a proposition I would accept? If you are, don't be. Let me give you the case history of Doris Lamar in capsule form."

She leaned back in her chair and crossed her knees. When she saw the exposed length of calf and thigh she flipped the kimono expertly to cover them. She sucked smoke into her lungs, blew it out, and watched it evaporate above her. Without make-up her face seemed younger somehow, but the lines of weariness remained at the corners of her mouth even though it twisted now into a half-smile.

"The name is really Doris Lasowitz and I grew up, if you could call it that, in a small town in West Virginia. Seven kids. A hard-working, worn-out mother, a father who never seemed able to earn quite enough money to take care of his own thirst and the food we needed. I was in my last year of high school when I got a chance to get out and I took it. I ran away with a boy who was three years older than I was. We got married."

She made a small, throaty sound in deprecation of the mental picture she had drawn and her mouth twisted.

"Some marriage. It lasted a year. At seventeen I was a bride and at eighteen-and-a-half I was a pregnant widow. My husband was killed by a cop in Pennsylvania when he tried to hold up a liquor store, and I suppose I got a break in a way because I wasn't with him. If I had been sitting in the car just then I probably would have done a few years in the penitentiary."

She put out her cigarette and continued in the same sardonic tone. "I tried marriage again at twenty-three, this time to a musician of all people. This one lasted three years, and while I got the divorce, the reason we couldn't work it out was probably more my fault than his. You see there were a lot of things wrong with Doris Lamar. I guess I never learned that in order to get anything worthwhile you have to give out. No one had bothered to teach me the fundamentals. I was lazy, selfish, greedy, and always looking for the easy way. When I discovered there wasn't any easy way there was nothing to do but keep working. I didn't have enough education to be much of a success in an office, so what was I? Waitress, barmaid, shill, hostess. You name it, Mr. Hayden.

"I'll be thirty-one my next birthday. I have a twelve-year-old son who's been living with foster parents in upstate New York for a long time. No charity, you understand. I've been sending a monthly check and that's another reason why I never seem to get a stake. But this winter I did some thinking because, except for George, there wasn't much else to do in a place like this. I started going to school in Bridgeport four mornings a week. English and typing. That was the extent of my ambition, and those bus trips were a real drag. I dropped out a month or so ago when I saw how George felt about me and guessed what he had in mind."

"What about Adler?" He paused and watched the half-smile fade. "You weren't in love with him, were you?"

"No."

"Then there must have been some money involved."

"There was."

"How much?" he said, still probing.

"He said he had a deal on that would bring him a minimum of ten thousand dollars and probably twenty. When he collected he was going to take off for Florida and he wanted me to go with him." She stopped, glanced at her wrist watch, and then jumped to her feet. "I've got to dress," she said. "You can talk from the doorway if you want to."

She went into the bedroom and he sat for a minute or two, seeing her toss the kimono onto the bed as she stepped out of sight. He could hear a closet door open and the clatter of metal coat hangers. When she reappeared again she had on a simple black dress, which was her costume at Jerry's Tavern, and now she sat down on the edge of the bed and drew on her stockings. There was no hint of self-consciousness in the act and her movements were swift and practiced. When she stood again and shook her dress down he started toward the doorway. She was sitting on a bench and facing a rickety-looking vanity as he leaned against the doorframe. She began to work on her face and he said:

"Did Adler say where he was going to get this money?"

"No, but—I'm only guessing about this—I got the idea that maybe you had something to do with it."

"You would have gone with him?"

"I think so. I've known a lot of men like Sam Adler. I could have handled him all right. Maybe to someone like you this doesn't make much sense. Maybe you think I should have stayed here and married George Freeman, and maybe you're right. The way things turned out I'm sure you're right, but I saw this chance to get my hand on some money and maybe a new start in Florida. Adler didn't talk me into anything; I talked myself into it. George is forty years old but he acts like a kid about a lot of things—"

"You could probably change that."

She looked up at him then and the lipstick she had been working with remained poised in mid-air. "Do you really think so?"

Hayden said he did, then added: "Adler asked you a lot of questions about me, didn't he?"

"Well, a few anyway."

"He asked you if you knew me, and where I lived, and what I was doing, and how was I making out."

"That's right."

"He gave you the idea that he expected to make some deal with me but he didn't tell you what it was."

"No."

"Did he mention my wife?"

"I don't think so."

As he considered her reply he had an idea that he had learned all he was going to learn about this particular subject, so he mentioned the other thing that had been bothering him.

"You weren't at Jerry's when I went in there for a drink around a quarter of nine, were you?"

"No."

"Where were you?"

"I've told the police a half a dozen times, so I might as well tell you," she said dryly. "I had a splitting headache. I get them every so often and I have some prescription pills a doctor gave me. Last night I forgot them and I stood it as long as I could, and then I asked Jerry if I could come over here and get them. He said sure and I came. I was gone maybe twenty-five minutes or so."

She stood up as she finished, collected the soiled tissues, and dropped them into the wastebasket. She examined herself in the mirror and gave a final pat to her blond hair and then, as though all this had been nothing more than a polite social conversation, she changed the subject.

"Could you give me a lift to the tavern, please? I'd rather be a few minutes early than walk."

This told Hayden that he had gone about as far as he could. He said he would be glad to give her a ride, and not until they were in the car and he had started the motor did he make his final proposition. He did not believe he had heard all the truth. This was a woman who had learned a lot about life and was experienced in its ways. She had learned to be devious as a matter of self-protection, but she could not be expected to involve herself in unrewarding situations, particularly when they might involve her personally. On the other hand she had proved that she could be tempted by money, and it was with this thought in mind that he made his proposition.

"Sam Adler made you a proposition which you accepted because you thought it was going to pay off. Now I'll make one. I think you know more about this murder than you'll admit—"

"Now, wait a minute," she said, resentment showing for the first time in her voice.

"Hear me out," Hayden said. "If you've told all you know I can't very well make a proposition, but if you can help me find out who killed Adler I'd be willing to pay you for your help."

"You mean some kind of a deal just between you and me?"

"Yes."

"Like a reward?"

"Something like that."

"Have you got any special figure in mind?"

"I was thinking of something between one and five thousand dollars, depending on how much good your help does. You could keep it in mind."

"I will. I can tell you now I don't know who killed Sam, but if I think of anything that seems important I'll let you know."

Hayden wanted to tell her that she didn't have to know who killed Adler. All she had to do was come up with something that would clear Marion and, if possible, himself. Since he could not put such thoughts into words he simply told her to keep thinking.

CHAPTER 10

DRIVING HOME AFTER DROPPING Doris Lamar at the tavern, John Hayden reviewed what had been said and what he had accomplished. The results, as he saw them, were discouraging.

The admission that Adler had come here to collect a large sum of money and that she might have been willing to leave town with him in the hope of getting some of that money only confirmed what he already knew. He did not think she was telling the whole truth and he had wanted to put more pressure on her, to speak of the woman he had seen in the darkened quadrangle and to accuse her of being that woman. Yet, even as the thought had come to him, he knew that he could not carry out the threat because to do so would be to admit that he had also been there at the time.

The thought continued to disturb him, and when he turned his car into the driveway and saw the three cars parked in front of the house he found a new source of concern. For the plain black sedan with its buggy-whip antenna told him this was probably an unmarked police car. The convertible, he knew, belonged to Roger Denham. The third car, a two-toned sedan, was not familiar and he wondered about it as he walked through the breezeway and kitchen to the living room.

His first impression was that the room was crowded, and his glance moved to his wife, who was sitting in her accustomed chair at one side of the fireplace. He saw at once that the high-cheekboned face was composed but the hazel eyes were veiled and he could not read them as he leaned down and kissed her on the cheek. He was aware that the five men in the room had come to their feet, and when he understood that Marion did not seem unduly disturbed, he turned to face them, his resentment mounting. He was about to give voice to it when Roger Denham spoke up to interrupt him.

"John—this is Fred Erickson, the State's Attorney." He indicated the stocky, square-faced man in his middle forties who had a crew-cut and dark-rimmed glasses. "And Paul Simpson." He nodded to a younger man who had been sitting off to one side, a slender, black-haired fellow who was casually clad in flannel slacks and a checked sport jacket that was a little on the loud side. "Mr. Simpson is with the Allied Insurance Company."

Hayden made no attempt to shake hands nor did the others. He looked at Denham with his conservative but expensive-looking business suit, at the lean, competent figure of Lieutenant Garvey, at the round, impassive, and steady-eyed face of County Detective Ball.

"Well," he said, with no trace of cordiality, "since you're here you might as well sit down. I don't know what you have in mind, but it seems to me that instead of coming here and ganging up on my wife you could have waited—"

Marion cut in before he could finish. "That's not the way it happened, darling," she said. "When I talked to you this noon you said you'd be home early. Roger called and said these men would like to talk to us and I told him it would be all right. I thought you'd be here before they came."

"We thought it would be more convenient for both of you," Erickson added, "to talk here instead of in my office."

The simple explanation should have mollified Hayden but his initial annoyance remained and his voice was still curt.

"Okay, so what do you want from us?"

Before Erickson could reply, Simpson spoke up. "I'm here on my own, Mr. Hayden. If you don't mind my waiting I'd like to talk to you a few minutes when these gentlemen have finished."

Hayden made no reply. He was still watching the State's Attorney, who studied him for a silent moment before he said: "We've had some information that leads us to believe that Mrs. Hayden's first husband may still be alive."

So that's how it is, Hayden thought bitterly.

He was not yet prepared to grapple with the problem, and the top of his mind suggested an answer and he grabbed it. Aside from Adler only he, Marion, and Denham knew of Adler's contention that Ted Corbin was still alive. He was positive that Marion would never speak of this knowledge to anyone. That left Denham, and in the momentary silence that followed the State's Attorney's remark, his sudden dislike for the lawyer was a corrosive force that influenced his thinking. Little things that had bothered him before, over the past year or so, came quickly to mind and he tabulated them swiftly.

Denham, it seemed, had never liked him. Denham, with his top social background and inherited money and his fine education. The bespectacled eyes that met his seemed calm and unconcerned, and he was reminded again of Denham's ascetic looks and manner of living, his abstinence, the credo of physical fitness, with strenuous squash in the winter and even more strenuous tennis in the summer.

In fairness, he had to admit that Denham was no pantywaist. He had proved that in Korea when he was a member of a Ranger unit. He had been decorated for bravery because of something he had done while leading a night patrol, and this was something Hayden could not minimize even now. But Denham had been a suitor of sorts, an unsuccessful one where Marion was concerned. He had not liked Ted Corbin; he did not like John Hayden, and this was his way of paying them back and....

He heard the State's Attorney clear his throat, and as he shifted his gaze and saw what the man had in his hand he could only stare while a feeling of shame came over him and he understood how unfair he had been in his thoughts of Denham. For he saw now that Erickson had a small photograph in his hand. Even from where he sat, and without moving closer, he seemed to understand that this was a copy of the one he now had in his pocket. Denham had not given the show away, but he still could not imagine how Erickson could have got such a picture, and he sat silently until the explanation came.

"Lieutenant Garvey got Adler's address from a driving license," he said. "He got in touch with the Mobile police—it was an Alabama license with a Mobile address—last night and they got right on it."

He held the picture with extended fingers and Hayden understood that he was to take it. He did so; he looked at it. He glanced at Marion, but she was busy drawing an imaginary line on the arm of the chair with her index finger.

"Has my wife seen this?" he said, returning the picture.

"She says it's a picture of her first husband." Erickson slipped the photograph back into his pocket. "Adler was a small-time gambler and con man who followed the horses. He moved about a lot, but he kept this apartment in Mobile as his headquarters. The Mobile police had a file on him—nothing impressive—gambling, disorderly conduct, things like that. Naturally they searched his apartment and apparently they searched it well. They found this envelope. It had two negatives and two prints. They didn't know what they meant but Garvey thought they might be important. The other photograph showed the fingerprints of a man's right hand."

He leaned back on the divan and said: "To save time the Mobile people put the two pictures in an envelope and gave it to a steward on a morning flight out of Mobile. They figured this would be quicker than using the mails. We sent a man down to Idlewild and he picked up the envelope. We don't know about the fingerprints yet—they're being checked in Washington and we'll probably know by tomorrow—but it's a reasonable assumption that those prints will belong to Mrs. Hayden's first husband."

"What did my wife say about the picture you just showed me?" Hayden asked evenly.

"She says she doesn't know when it was taken. She implies that it might have been done several years ago."

Hayden's immediate reply was a grunt that was audible, disparaging, and slightly contemptuous.

"Ted Corbin was killed in a plane crash more than two years ago," he said. "There was no doubt about his death at the time and I don't think there's any doubt now. The fact that Mr. Simpson's company paid off the insurance claim should be proof enough."

"I'm aware of that," Erickson said calmly, "but stranger things than that have happened. You understand I'm making no accusation, nor am I asking for a definite statement from you at this time. But I'd like to draw you a hypothetical picture that seems to me to have some merit."

"Before you do," Hayden said, "tell me a little about George Freeman. Freeman had a very good motive for murder—you must know about that—and he also had the opportunity. I suppose you questioned him?"

"Until two o'clock last night," Ball said.

"And for three hours again this morning," Garvey added.

"Does he have an alibi?"

"No," Erickson said. "He maintains that he was in the motel office from shortly after seven until he found Adler at around nine-thirty."

"Did he just happen to find him?"

"He admits he was jealous. He was afraid Doris Lamar might be thinking about running off with Adler. He'd been brooding the night before and all that day, and he finally decided to go down to Adler's room and have it out with him. He got no answer when he knocked but the lights were on and he could hear the radio playing and Adler's rented car was there. When he could get no reply to his knock he was too upset to give up, so he used his passkey and unlocked the door. He found Adler on the floor and called the State Police.... Now if you don't mind, Mr. Hayden," he added, "let me get back to my hypothesis."

He paused to be sure there would be no interruption and said: "Adler, who was a known gambler and confidence man, comes to Morrisville the day before yesterday. He makes inquiries at the gas station and Jerry's Tavern about John Hayden. He wants to know where you live, what you do, and how you're doing. Why?"

"It's your hypothesis," Hayden said coldly.

"On the basis of these two pictures which came from Mobile, it suggests that your wife's first husband is still alive. Otherwise there would be no point in Adler coming here since he had nothing to sell. We know that he *did* come to this house and he *did* talk to your wife. She maintains that he represented himself as a book salesman and yet there was no physical evidence on Adler's person, the motel room, or his car to support any such contention. Book salesmen simply don't go around without samples, or at least without some advertising literature describing the books."

Marion stirred in her chair and Hayden was a little amazed that she could make her rebuttal sound so calm and disinterested. "I saw no books and no literature," she said. "I only know what he said."

"Freeman says that Adler made a call to this number," Erickson continued. "You deny you received such a call." He turned his attention to Hayden. "You went to Mr. Denham's house at eight o'clock for a meeting of some kind. Mr. Denham, as your attorney, has refused to discuss the substance of your conversation and he cannot be forced to do so at this time. He says you left around eight-thirty and that he understood you were going to stop at the tavern and get a drink before you went home."

Hayden gave Denham another good mark for his loyalty and circumspection as he said: "And that's exactly what I did."

"You were seen to leave the tavern and walk in the direction of the motel but you say your car was parked there. You got in and drove directly here."

"That's right."

"My hypothesis suggests another possibility. It indicates that Adler came to Morrisville with blackmail on his mind. He came to see Mrs. Hayden, not to sell books but to offer proof that her first husband was still alive. Since we know that there were two negatives and two prints in his Mobile apartment it seems reasonable to assume that he brought an extra set of prints with him to substantiate his claim."

He hesitated, his gaze moving from Hayden to Marion and back again. "It's useless to speculate at this point as to how Adler knew that Mr. Corbin escaped that fatal plane crash, but the only logical assumption is that he never boarded that plane. If Adler knew this much, he could also know that the insurance companies paid seventy-five thousand dollars to your wife on the death claim. He wanted some of that money and he was willing to keep silent for a price.

"Following this assumption, I suggest that you went to see Mr. Denham to get his advice. Whatever the outcome of that discussion, you went to the tavern and from there to room twelve in The Shady Maple Motel. You either entered that room and had an argument which resulted in Adler's death or you went in and found him already dead."

"You said the door was locked."

"Either way," Erickson said, as though he had not heard, "you found the two photographs Adler had brought and destroyed them. Had it not been for the alertness of the Mobile police, there would not be the slightest reason for us to assume that your wife's first husband was still alive."

"It's a good hypothesis," Hayden said, "but it doesn't happen to be true."

"Very well." Erickson rose and the movement brought Garvey and Ball to their feet. "When we get word from Washington tomorrow about those fingerprints we'll start looking for Ted Corbin. Because of his connection with that fatal plane crash we may get some help from the FBI." He glanced at the insurance man who had been listening to all this attentively. "I have an idea Mr. Simpson's company will utilize their resources as well."

"They sure will, sir," Simpson said.

Hayden watched the trio put on their coats and pick up their hats. He knew he was expected to say something but nothing came to mind. This silence seemed to increase the State's Attorney's frustration and his mouth was tight and his eyes grim as he delivered his final statement.

"We will need a statement from you as soon as we hear from Washington. A formal statement, Mr. Hayden. One that you will be expected to sign and which may be used against you."

Hayden nodded. He said that he would do whatever Roger Denham told him to do and started for the front door. When he opened it the three filed out without further comment.

Back in the living room Denham and Simpson were on their feet and Denham said: "You've probably had your fill of questions for one afternoon, John, but I think you ought to hear what Mr. Simpson has to say."

"I haven't any hypothesis, Mr. Hayden," Simpson said, "but I have to make an assumption."

"That Ted Corbin is alive?"

Simpson nodded and gestured with one hand. "Naturally nothing can be done until we have the facts, but if it happens that we do locate Corbin, my company will expect to be reimbursed for the payment made to your wife."

"In full?"

Simpson's brows lifted. "How do you mean?"

"That seventy-five thousand was paid to my wife in good faith and she accepted it in good faith. She later turned that money over to me and I put it into my business. Suppose I couldn't raise that amount all at once?"

"We could probably get a judgment."

"That would be something for Mr. Denham to handle," Hayden said. "But let me ask you a question." He offered a small, humorless smile. "A hypothetical one again. Suppose that someone came to you and offered to prove that Corbin was alive. Suppose they offered to produce him for a price. To get a chance at recovering your seventy-five thousand you would pay pretty well for that information, wouldn't you?"

"That would depend on a lot of things, but offhand I'd say yes, we would pay for that sort of information." Simpson tipped his head slightly and one brow lifted. "Oh, I see what you mean. You think the seventy-five thousand dollars should be reduced by whatever amount we might have paid to get the information we need."

"Something like that," Hayden said. "Mr. Denham will have to do the negotiating, but if Corbin is located I'll try to reimburse your company to the best of my ability. I'd simply like to get the best deal I can."

"I have no authority to make deals," Simpson said, "but I can give my superiors the picture. I could tell them that you would be willing to repay the amount less, say, ten per cent."

"Let's not get into figures yet," Denham said. "You find Corbin and we'll work something out."

Simpson reached for his coat and hat. "Don't think we won't try. All I wanted to do today was to get some idea about Mr. Hayden's attitude."

"You've got it," Denham said.

"Fair enough." Simpson nodded to Hayden and to Marion. "Thanks for your co-operation.... Good-by, Mrs. Hayden...."

When Simpson had gone Roger Denham put on his coat. Hayden, feeling the reaction in his muscles, watched his wife stand up, and now, with no need to maintain an outward display of composure, the strain was beginning to show on her face and her mouth was slack.

"What are we going to do, Roger?"

"Nothing for now, I'm afraid."

"What about those statements the State's Attorney spoke of?"

"Well"—Denham shrugged—"you'll have to make them. Naturally, I'll be there with you, but I think there's one thing you might as well start getting used to."

"What's that?" Hayden said.

"I think Corbin is probably alive, and once the various law-enforcement agencies start looking for him, they'll find him. It will just be a question of time. That's what makes it bad. It could happen quickly. It might take years."

"Meanwhile," Marion said with undisguised bitterness, "we just go along as usual and pretend everything is all right."

"You do the best you can," Denham said as he started for the door, "and hope the police can find out who killed Adler. The sooner the better."

CHAPTER 11

JOHN HAYDEN STOOD IN the partly open door until the taillights on Denham's car vanished down the road, and when he came back to the living room Marion was still standing. He could see that reaction had begun to relieve the tension which had been with her for so long, and this, he told himself, was a good sign. There was a little color in her cheeks now, and when she repeated the question she had asked Denham, her voice no longer sounded so disconsolate.

"Well," she said, "at least they've gone. But what do we do now?"

"Get a drink."

"All right. I'll get the ice."

He slid his arm around her waist as they went into the kitchen. He stopped her for a moment before she turned toward the refrigerator. He said he was proud of her.

"You were wonderful."

"Was I, John?" She glanced up at him, the hazel eyes softly shining. "I tried awfully hard. But so were you, the way you talked to that State's Attorney. He didn't like it though, did he?... I think I'll have a Scotch and soda."

He made the drinks and they sat down in the kitchen alcove. When he had a cigarette going he took out the photograph of Ted Corbin, his mind busy now with an idea that until then had been nothing more than a vague and nebulous possibility. His frown deepened as the seconds passed, and presently she covered his hand with hers to claim his attention.

"What are you thinking about?"

"Him." He touched the picture.

"What about him?"

"I'm going to look for him."

"For Ted? Where?"

"In Mobile. That's where Adler made his headquarters. I think it's the best place to start."

He could tell that she thought the suggestion was farfetched. A frown made little bunches in the smooth brow and her eyes were puzzled as they inspected him. But she did not belittle the thought and her reply was rational and intelligent.

"How big is Mobile?"

"I don't know. I've never been there. As a guess I'd say a couple hundred thousand."

"And won't the Mobile police be looking for Ted?"

"I should think so."

"And the insurance people?"

"Sure."

"Then what makes you think you could find him, even assuming that he's there, before they do?"

"Maybe I can't but I think it's worth a try. See that?" He pointed at the photograph and her eyes followed his finger as he indicated the insignia on the coveralls Ted Corbin wore. "See that insignia? Suppose I can get this picture blown up—"

"Blown up?"

"I can get it copied. I can have an enlargement made from the new negative. I think there's a good chance that we may be able to read the words on that insignia."

"Oh—"

"It's possible, isn't it? If this picture was taken fairly recently, and according to Adler it was, Corbin must be working in some filling station. If he's in that area, I've got an idea I can locate it. If I can do that, I can find him."

She did not ask him how but the frown was still there and her eyes were thoughtful now. "And what would you do if you did find him, John?"

"Do? I'd try and talk him into coming back with me."

"Why should he?"

"I don't see that he has much choice. If he doesn't want to do it that way, all I have to do is pick up the telephone and call the Mobile police."

She was still watching him intently but concern had now replaced the thoughtfulness in her eyes and this was reflected in the cadence of her voice.

"You mean you'd go now?"

"Tonight, if I can get out."

"But—what about the police? I mean the State's Attorney and those two detectives? They'll think you've run away. Won't that make it look as if you were guilty?"

"Of stabbing Adler?"

"Well—yes."

"Maybe," he said, "but I intend to leave word where I've gone and why—after I've gone.... Come on, drink up."

She obeyed him and then, digressing, said: "I haven't done anything about dinner."

"We'll eat out. I'll find a place where we're not known. All you have to do is put on a coat and you'll be ready. I'll call Johnson and see—"

"Who's Johnson?"

"A photographer. He does most of our work down at the plant—you know, for advertising folders. He's got a studio in South Norwalk, and if I can reach him I think he'll make a copy of this print and then make the sort of enlargement I want. If I'm right and that picture can be blown up so that we can read what's on that insignia I'm going to Mobile.

"But first I'm going into the study and get that portable typewriter of mine and write a note to State's Attorney Erickson with a carbon to Roger Denham. I'll simply tell them that I'm not running away. I'll point out that I have an idea I can locate Corbin, that whether I do or whether I don't, I'll be back in a couple of days. Let them think what they want. I can mail those letters special delivery. I can drive to New York, leave the car in a garage, and get a taxi to the airport and—"

"I'll go with you."

"No, you won't."

"I don't mean to Mobile. But why can't I drive you into town?"

"No."

"But I want to. Please, John. It will be much simpler that way and then you won't have to worry about the car.... You go ahead," she added quickly as though to forestall further argument. "You call your man Johnson and I'll get your typewriter ready and some paper and carbon."

Hayden had no trouble getting Johnson to take the after-hours assignment. He had a small studio in back of his house and Marion waited in the station wagon while the work was being done. It did not take long because Johnson made his enlargement from the wet negative on which he had copied the original snapshot. Hayden left this negative with the photographer, and when he came back to the car he had the original print and a second one that had been cropped to show only the upper part of Corbin's coveralls. The insignia which had been sewn there was fuzzy but readable and showed a star with the word Quinn above it and Cannon below.

They stopped in town to mail the two letters Hayden had written and they had dinner at a small restaurant not far from the parkway. While Marion was having her coffee Hayden stepped into the phone booth and called the

New York Airlines Terminal to find out what he could about flights to Mobile. When he came back to the table he said that there were two which would do.

"Both are out of Newark. One is at one-thirty—"

"In the morning? What time would you get there?"

"Around five-thirty."

"What about the other one?"

"I'd have to stay in New York overnight. It leaves at nine-thirty in the morning, but it's a jet with only one stop and puts me into Mobile a little after one in the afternoon."

"Take that one," Marion said with no hesitation. "The other way you sit up all night without any sleep and then when you get there you have to wait around until the middle of the morning before you can expect to find out anything."

What she said made sense. He might waste a couple of hours that way, but he would be rested when he got to Mobile and ready to start looking for a service station that apparently was run by people named Quinn and Cannon. He said he had reservations on both flights and would confirm the morning flight when he got to New York, but as they got into the car he voiced his doubts about her determination to accompany him to the city.

"You really shouldn't come at all," he said.

"I'd like to know why not."

"Furthermore," he added, "I'm running out on you when things are toughest. That State's Attorney is bound to question you tomorrow and you'll have to take it alone."

"What makes you think I can't?" She pushed her chin out at him a fraction of an inch and her mouth was determined. "And anyway I won't be alone. Roger will be there. All I have to do is repeat what I've already told those detectives."

"And what about me?"

"I'll say you packed a bag and made me drive you to the railroad station. I'll say you said you'd be gone a couple of days and told me not to worry. You refused to tell me where you were going; you simply left. How can anyone prove otherwise?"

Her reply reassured him and helped to bolster his own determination to follow this one lead he had in the hope that it would take him to Ted Corbin. He knew how his disappearance would look; he had to admit his trip might be both ill-timed and futile. Even so it seemed worth the risk, and her spirit and co-operation reminded him again of how much he loved her.

"Okay," he said. "Just stick to that."

"I intend to.... Where will you stay tonight?"

He said he would pick some hotel not too far from the West Side Terminal and she accepted this as they came up on the parkway and headed toward the city. For a few minutes then nothing more was said and he gave his attention to his driving. This soon became automatic, and with his mind free to think again, he reluctantly examined a thought that had lodged there the night before and continued to fester ever since. He was not sure this was the time to bring the thought out into the open. He was worried about how she might take it, but he knew he would worry even more if he left without knowing the truth. He reached out with his right hand until he found her knee. He squeezed it gently and she put her hand on top of his. He took a deep breath and decided he was as ready as he ever would be.

"I have to ask you something before you drop me off," he said. "I don't want to but I haven't any choice, baby. Where did you go last night after I went to see Roger?"

The silence that followed alarmed him. At first he wondered if she had heard him and then, when she removed her hand from the back of his own, he knew she had. She moved her knee and he put his hand back on the steering wheel. When she finally spoke her voice was small and uncertain.

"I—I'm not sure what you mean. What makes you think I went anywhere?"

He told her how he had come into the garage the night before and stumbled in the darkness when he started for the light switch.

"I put my hand on the hood of the station wagon to get my balance," he said. "It was warm. The radiator shell was even warmer. It was a fairly cold night."

"I see," she said in the same small voice. "And all this time you've been thinking I went to see Adler."

"I didn't know what to think. I guess I was afraid to ask. Look, sweetheart, I'm not the State's Attorney, I'm your husband. This is something we have to work out together."

"I didn't want to worry you. I wasn't going to say anything about it."

"You told me Adler called you. So what, exactly, did he want?"

"Just about what I told you before. He said he wanted to see me. I told him that you were probably on your way there and he said that was all right too. He said maybe it would be better if the three of us talked things over together. I guess that's why I decided to go."

Hayden did not understand what she meant. He said so.

"I was afraid," she said in an effort to explain. "Not for myself, for you."

"For me?" he said in slow astonishment.

"Because I was afraid of what might happen. You have to try to understand—"

"I *am* trying."

"You don't know how you looked when you left the house to see Roger. You don't get angry very often. Hardly ever. But what I saw was something more than anger. If you could have got your hands on Adler then I don't know what you would have done. I didn't think talking to Roger would help much and you had never seen Adler; you didn't know what he was like. He could be arrogant and insulting and impossible. I thought if I was there when you came, at least there wouldn't be any violence."

"All right," he said, accepting the explanation and trying to bring some order to his thoughts. "I'm not criticizing. I'm not blaming you. I just want to find out what happened."

"Nothing happened," she said, her voice forlorn. "I wasn't there long enough. I knew the minute I walked in that it had been a mistake to come."

"What did he do?"

"Nothing much. He offered me a drink. He said that women always liked Tom Collinses and he was about to make one. He started to squeeze a lemon—"

Hayden interrupted as a new thought came to him. "Did you see him cut that lemon?"

"Yes."

"Where did he get the knife?"

"I think he took it from a cabinet drawer."

"What did he do with it after he finished?"

"Well, I guess he put it back."

"All right," he said, not wanting her to think too much about his questions. "He offered you a drink. Then what?"

"I told him I didn't want one. He came over to help me off with my coat. I told him I'd leave it on, but he must have thought I wanted to be coaxed.... Oh, why do I have to explain all the details?" she cried, a break in her voice. "I simply couldn't stand him. I knew I'd been a fool to come at all. I pushed him away and got out of there as fast as I could."

"That's all?"

"I think it's more than enough."

"Okay, okay. It's over now. You went there because you thought you could be of some help to me. When you realized it was a bad idea you got out. Now did anyone see you?"

"Not that I know of."

"Where did you park?"

"Around the corner."

"Good. Then there's nothing to worry about."

"Nothing to worry about?" she said in quick exasperation. "How can you say that?"

"I mean, if no one saw you how can anyone suspect you?"

"They suspect you, don't they?"

"Yes, I guess they do."

"Then unless the police find out who *did* kill Adler they'll keep right on suspecting both of us."

"They'll find out," he said with a confidence he did not feel. "They usually do."

"I don't even see how finding Ted is going to help. He might even have sent Adler."

"Whoa!" He again reached out and found her knee. He squeezed it. "Take it easy. Let the police worry about the murder. Just hope I get to Corbin and bring him back. You and he and I have some things to straighten out, remember?"

There was no reply to this, and as he turned off the West Side highway at Fifty-seventh Street he could feel her shoulder relax against his. A corner street light cast its rays momentarily on her face and he saw that she was watching him. He could not read her eyes but her mouth looked soft and he thought she was trying to smile.

"I'm sorry I got so worked up, darling," she said. "I've been worried sick. I wanted to tell you before but I was afraid to."

"I'm glad you did." He made the turn on Ninth Avenue and started slowly south, his glance inspecting the lighted rooftop signs until he saw a hotel he had heard of but never patronized. He pointed it out to her as he made a left turn and started crosstown toward Seventh Avenue. He said he guessed he'd try it and she said why not, and was he sure he had everything he needed?

The question prompted him to review his hurried preparations. He was purposely traveling light because he felt he would succeed quickly or not at all. The overnight case contained clean linen, an extra pair of shoes, a robe, neckties, handkerchiefs. The blue-fabric flight bag held his toilet kit, pajamas, and a clean shirt.

He did not have as much cash as he wanted, but what he had in his wallet and what Marion had in the house came to just under two hundred dollars. Credit cards would take care of most everything, but to use them meant to give his right name, and since he did not know how long it would be before the police started looking for him, he intended to use a fictitious name at the hotel and at the airport and pay cash.

He told her he thought he was all set. He said she was not to worry about him. He said he would telephone her when he could and the sound of his words seemed to give him new confidence. Somehow he was no longer disturbed by what he was about to do; instead his concern was directed at his wife.

The thought of her driving home alone did not bother him greatly because she was both skillful and experienced behind the wheel of a car. But the thought of her spending the night alone in an empty house, and of the questioning and suspicion that was sure to follow tomorrow, depressed him and he said so as he pulled the station wagon into the curb opposite the hotel marquee.

"You're sure you're going to be all right?"

"Quite sure."

"Do you know what you're going to say tomorrow?"

"Of course I do."

"Promise me you'll drive home carefully."

"I promise."

He opened the door and stepped to the sidewalk, pointing out the two bags to the doorman who hurried up to help. He closed the door and leaned in the open window as she slid over on the seat, and before he realized it she had her arms around his neck and was kissing him soundly. She seemed, for the moment, to have forgotten her compunctions about the legality of their marriage, and as she pressed her cheek hard against his her words fell softly in his ear.

"Good-by, my darling. I wish I was staying with you tonight."

"Yeah," he said, so surprised and moved by her reaction that his voice came out husky. He had to swallow to clear his throat before he could repeat the word. "Yeah. Me too.... Drive carefully," he said and stepped back as she put the car in gear and angled out into the moving traffic stream.

CHAPTER 12

FLIGHT 303 OUT OF Newark departed on time on Thursday morning and made its scheduled stop at Atlanta shortly after noon. The trip was high, smooth, and surprisingly quiet, and John Hayden, who had brought two morning papers aboard with him, had occupied himself with a careful reading of both of them. Nowhere could he find any reference to a follow-up story on Sam Adler's death, and he felt sure that if a search was to be made for him, it had not started the night before.

Lunch was served as soon as the aircraft was again airborne, and by the time he had finished—he had a window seat now on the starboard side—he could tell that the pilot had already begun to lose altitude in his approach to Mobile. The land beneath the wingtip seemed gently rolling now, with cultivated areas interspersed with stands of pine. For the past few minutes they had flown over one river after another, each seemingly flowing southward toward the gulf or bay, but he was hazy about his geography in that area and he could only identify those which were shown on the airline map—the Alabama first, the Tensaw, the Mobile.

The position of the sun and his long-forgotten Boy Scout training told him that they were flying more west than southwest now. He thought they were down to probably four or five thousand feet when the pilot banked gently and the starboard wing lifted. When they were again in level flight they were lower and the direction had been reversed and he understood that they were about to approach Bates Field from the west. He could see no signs of the city, but the flaps were down now and they came down over the low plateau to touch the concrete runway with a moderate bump and a small squeal of rubber as the tires took their weight.

The sky was bright and cloudless as he walked toward the small but modern-looking terminal building, and the sun brought a welcome warmth to the air. He thought the temperature was in the middle seventies, perhaps more, and as he waited at the baggage counter he slipped off his topcoat and draped it over his arm.

There were fifteen or twenty passengers in all and it did not take long to claim his overnight bag. This required no porter and he went past the glass doors to the interior, scanning the waiting room, the newsstand and souvenir shop, the air-conditioned restaurant. There were two car-rental agencies on opposite sides of the hall, one with some newly arrived customers and one without. Since he had no preference he headed for the latter and stated his needs.

"Yes, sir," the agent said. "May I see your driver's license and some identification? Do you want to handle this with a credit card?"

Hayden, who had been listed on the passenger manifest as John Hastings, Hartford, Connecticut, produced two credit cards and the agent took his pick. Hayden said that a small sedan would do, that he probably would not need it for more than a couple of days. A form was filled out, the rates explained, and while Hayden signed it the agent picked up the telephone and spoke briefly. When he hung up he glanced again at the application form, removed the carbons, and gave Hayden a copy.

"Thank you, Mr. Hayden," he said. "Now all you have to do is drive."

"Do you happen to have any kind of map of the city?"

The man said he had. He said it was not too detailed but it would give Hayden the main streets and the principal points of interest. He reached under the counter, handed over the map, and pointed toward the opposite end of the terminal.

"If you just wait out there at the ramp your car will be right along."

Hayden saw the small green sedan coming as he stopped outside under the covered driveway, and as he waited a young Negro negotiated the curve with a flourish, stopped smoothly, and jumped out to get the bags.

"Put them in the rear deck, sir?"

"The back seat will do."

"Right." The youth got rid of the bags, took the topcoat, folded it neatly. "There you are, sir."

"How do I get out of here?" Hayden said and reached for a coin.

"To Mobile? Just follow that." He pointed to a road that ran along the plateau between two high wire fences. "You come to the end, you turn left."

"How far?"

"Maybe ten miles, straight in."

When Hayden turned left at the intersection on the perimeter of the field he found himself on a narrow, two-lane highway that stretched straight ahead over gently rolling country. Tall pine trees bordered the road here, and beyond were fields and an occasional house. Traffic was moderate, but as he continued, filling stations began to appear with increasing frequency. Roadside stands and small stores soon gave way to larger ones. Traffic increased and the rolling terrain made passing more difficult as the area began to take on a suburban look. Here and there were real estate developments which optimists had laid out with an eye to the future, but after he had passed a large shopping center the section had a more permanent look and the pines gave way to oaks and magnolias and camphor trees.

By now both sides of the road were built up, and he came finally to a broad thoroughfare, angling into it at a traffic light. After that the highway was divided and thick with cars. Ancient and enormous live oaks sent out branches that nearly met above the traffic, and as he stopped for a signal light he saw that he was on Government Street. When, a few blocks farther on, he noticed the new-looking, two-story motel on his right, he pulled in and coasted to a stop opposite the office.

At this hour he had no trouble getting accommodations, and once again he used a fictitious name and address as he registered and paid in advance for his room. A uniformed bellboy took the key and showed him where to park his car. He carried the bags to a second-floor unit that overlooked the swimming pool and asked if Hayden would like some ice. Hayden said no and tipped him, and when the door closed he took off his hat and sat down to do some thinking.

He did not bother to unpack but took out the snapshot of Ted Corbin. The familiar star in the background told him that this was a Texaco filling station and it had been his intention to find the local sales agency and start his quest from there. Now, realizing that he might be able to get the necessary information by telephone, he reached for the directory and gave the number to the motel operator.

A glance at his watch told him it was three o'clock, but he remembered that there was an hour's difference in time between Mobile and Newark. This made it two o'clock here, and he told himself hopefully that most of the office help should be back from lunch by now. When, a moment later, a woman answered, he asked to be connected to someone in the sales department.

Not until he had stated his request and heard the brief silence while the operator transferred his call did it occur to him that he ought to have a story to tell. For to come right out and ask directly for his information might result in some suspicion or a flat refusal, depending on company policy. The thought jarred him and he felt a moment of simple panic before he could make his mind work constructively. He was still grappling with the problem when a man's voice said: "Sales. McCann speaking."

With that he took a quick breath and knew that he could only make up a story as he went along and hope it sounded convincing.

"This is Mr. Hastings," he said. "The name won't mean anything to you but I'd like to get some information about one of your stations."

"What sort of information, Mr. Hastings?"

"My wife was here a couple of months ago and when she pulled into a station to get some gas one of the attendants found out that her motor was overheating. It was nothing serious—something about the fan belt, I think—but he fixed it for her and wouldn't take any payment for the favor. I don't know if it's one of your company stations or an independent, but since I'm going to be in town a couple of days I thought I'd like to stop at that station and get a tankful of gas and thank the man who helped her out that time."

"I'm glad we could be of service, Mr. Hastings," McCann said. "It's always nice to hear and I appreciate your thought about thanking the man personally. Does your wife remember the name of the station or where it was located?"

"She doesn't know where it was. She's not even sure it was in the city proper but she knows it was in the area. She didn't think to see who owned the place but she remembers the insignia on the man's coveralls. There was this star you use with the name Quinn above it and Cannon below. I thought maybe you'd have a station listed that was run by someone of that name."

He was perspiring freely when he finished and the back of his throat was dry. But his fabrication had sounded reasonable enough to his ears, and he felt a moment of exultation when the man said he would see what he could find. With that he crossed his fingers both mentally and physically and in the end his effort was rewarded.

"Mr. Hastings? There's no station in the city listed under those two names but there is one in Fairview."

"Fairview?"

"It's across the bay."

"I think it's worth a try," Hayden said. "How do I get there?"

"Where are you now?"

"In a motel on Government Street."

"That makes it easy. Stay right on Government. It'll take you through the Bankhead Tunnel and bring you out on the causeway. Bear right and follow the signs. Our station is right on Route 98 as you get into Fairview. I hope it's the one you want."

Hayden thanked the man and hung up, his spirits high and a sense of satisfaction taking charge of him that was hard to control. He clapped his hands absently and rubbed the palms. He uttered a happy curse, and when he caught sight of himself in the mirror he saw that his angular face had been warped into one huge grin. Taking only enough time to wash his hands and

face and comb his hair, he charged out of the room, pocketing his key and
slamming the door behind him.

CHAPTER 13

THE RIDE TO FAIRVIEW took no more than a half hour and in his frame of mind he found it enjoyable. The traffic down Government Street and through the tunnel did not bother him, and then he was on the divided causeway which cut across the top of Mobile Bay. Here there was a sixty-mile-an-hour speed limit and he looked with interest upon the low-lying borders and the fishermen, most of them Negroes, who dotted the shoreline a few feet from the road and tried their luck with long bamboo poles.

On the far shore the road curved right, and from then on he drove through wooded and somewhat hilly country, following the general line of the Bay but never actually catching sight of it. A high-standing, silvery water tower marked the town of Fairview before he saw it, and as he topped the last rise and saw the traffic lights ahead, he began to look for the filling station. The familiar star identified it almost at once. It stood on the left, but some impulse born of a caution he did not understand made him pull over to the right and stop while he considered his next step.

As it turned out, the enthusiasm which had brought him here proved to be short-lived. Because of his earlier success he had pictured himself as driving into the filling station, finding Ted Corbin, showing him the snapshot, and then playing the rest of it by ear. It had all seemed simple enough in concept, but as he sat there watching the filling station he began to have some doubts.

The physical layout of the station was of average size, with four pumps, rest rooms, twin grease racks adjacent to the office, and a parking area out back. The place was moderately busy, but a ten-minute inspection told him Corbin was not here.

Of the three men on duty, two were Negroes, one manning the gasoline pumps and the other busy greasing the car on one of the elevated racks. The third man was white, a stocky individual with a sunburned, weathered face who, when not busy, stood in the shade of the doorway and surveyed the passing scene.

There was a public telephone booth at one corner of the lot near the sidewalk, and Hayden left his car where it was and crossed diagonally to it. It did not seem likely that Corbin would still use the same name, but because he intended to overlook no possibilities, he stepped into the booth and consulted the telephone directory. When he found no Corbin listed either in Fairview or in the small nearby villages he knew that he would have to take his chances with the man in the doorway.

The man watched him approach, his dark gaze observant but noncommittal. He made no move to get out of the doorway until Hayden stopped in front of him and said: "Good afternoon."

"Afternoon, sir," came the reply in a voice that was deep and thick with accent.

"Do you have a cigarette machine?"

"In here." The man jerked his thumb and stepped aside.

"What do you put in?" Hayden asked, pleased to see that the insignia on the coveralls was identical with the one in the snapshot.

"Thirty cents for regulars."

Hayden looked for change and found he did not have the proper coins. He offered a dollar bill and the man punched the cash register, making change without comment. Hayden made his selection, dropped his coins, and pushed the release. The machine rattled and churned and a pack of cigarettes slid down on the shelf. By the time he had extracted one and put a light to it he knew that he might as well face up to his problem and get on with it. He found the snapshot, glanced at it. When he saw that he had the man's attention he passed it over.

"I think that was taken here," he said.

The man examined the picture, then turned it over as if he expected to find something on the back. When he was sure there was nothing to be seen he returned it, his weathered face impassive, the eyes inscrutable.

"Could be."

"Do you know him?"

"I might."

"Does he still work here?"

The man turned and spat on the ground. He gave a hitch to his coveralls and examined Hayden deliberately, his gaze steady but openly suspicious.

"What's your interest in him, friend?"

"Nothing very important," Hayden said. Then because he could think of no better story he repeated the one he had told earlier over the telephone.

He concentrated on keeping his tone casual, offhand, and friendly, but the reaction he got was disconcerting. There was, in fact, no reaction at all—just the same fixed expression and the uncompromising stare. In the face of this he found the going hard. The story that had seemed so reasonable before had a phony ring now and lacked conviction. Even so, the man heard him out.

"So your wife took his picture because he did her a favor. Well, I'm glad we could be of service." He held out his hand. "I'll give him the picture if you want."

Hayden put the snapshot back into his pocket but found some encouragement in the reply.

"Then he does work here?"

"Not right now. He's been North. I don't think he's back yet."

"Can you tell me where he lives?"

"I don't think so, mister."

With that Hayden gave up, but not without comment. Looking right at the man he said, a tight smile on his mouth and none at all in his eyes:

"You're a real trusting guy, aren't you—friend?"

For the first time the sunburned face cracked with a reluctant grin.

"Yes, sir—to my friends. Strangers have to prove themselves."

"Amen."

"What?"

"I said, thank you for your co-operation."

"You're welcome, friend.... Excuse me," he added and started for a car that had pulled up next to one of the gasoline pumps.

Hayden took a breath and expelled it with noisy exasperation. He knew he had gone as far as he could for the moment, but as he walked away his mind kept probing and he came up with another thought that seemed worth a try. It had been apparent that the filling station was run by two men named Quinn and Cannon. If his uncommunicative friend happened to be Quinn, then Cannon might be the name Ted Corbin had assumed. The initials were in themselves encouraging, and when he again examined the telephone directory in the public booth and found a T. J. Cannon listed, he went back to his car.

An inquiry at a corner drugstore gave him street directions, and he drove for five blocks to a small bungalow that stood back from the street and was shaded by oaks and magnolias. It had no distinction of any kind, a white stucco affair with the look of cheapness about it that seemed always to have been there. Over the years successive owners had provided a minimum of upkeep, the yard was scraggly and unkempt, but an air-conditioning unit poked its enclosed mechanism from a side window and there was a television antenna attached to the chimney.

There was no garage, but worn tracks spoke of a car that had been driven for some time to a resting place alongside the porch. There was no car now, but Hayden went up the path and knocked anyway. When he was sure no one was home, he drove back toward the center of town and parked diagonally across the street from the filling station, so that he could sit in comfort while he observed its operation.

As the afternoon wore on without any sign of the man he sought, his restlessness increased and his mood disintegrated with disheartening momentum. He realized then that he had been so encouraged by his original idea and his earlier success that he had expected too much too soon. Now he could only console himself with the thought that the original premise had been right: Corbin was alive. Corbin was here. With a proper show of patience he felt that all he had to do was wait long enough and Corbin would turn up.

But such idleness rankled. To combat it he let his thoughts move on until a new possibility suggested itself. Then, delaying no longer, he started the motor, drove around the block, and headed back toward Mobile.

For there was another man involved. Sam Adler had lived in Mobile and he remembered the Conti Street address he had copied down from the driving license that first night. Just what he might learn by having a look at Adler's local quarters he did not know, but as long as there was a chance that Cannon could be involved in the blackmail attempt there was also the possibility that he might learn something that would help shorten his search. He had no plans, nor did he bother to speculate. He would first locate the proper address, and after that he would see what developed.

He was in no hurry now, and the sun was almost down as he came out on the causeway and headed directly into its golden rays. Traffic was heavy on the other side of the highway as the city workers hurried home, but there was no congestion in his direction, and he had a chance to note the dry docks and shipyards on his left and the two freighters tied up at the Municipal Docks on his right beyond the Mobile River. Sunlight burnished two tall smokestacks in the distance. Their great height and the gray-white smoke that came from them to melt into the sky suggested that they might mark paper factories that had been built here to take advantage of the timber and the shipping facilities. Then he was turning off the causeway and paying his quarter and rolling through the relatively short and convenient tunnel that brought him into the heart of the city.

Once again on Government Street, he took the first right turn he could, aware from an earlier glance at the map that Conti Street was the next intersection, a one-way street that branched left. He saw as he made the turn that it was a narrow, unprepossessing street, the buildings that lined either side giving evidence that this was one of the older parts of town. After the first block or two, he found mostly small apartment houses and he slowed down, so that he could check the numbers.

He found the one he wanted two blocks farther on, a three-storied brick apartment with a discouraging outlook and a run-down appearance. He had to continue for nearly another block before he could pull into a parking place, and when he had locked the car he walked back to the entrance and stood a moment, wondering just how he should proceed. As he considered his problem a noise in the foyer beyond the open door attracted his attention and then he got a break.

A thin, wispy-haired man dressed in unpressed khaki slacks and a sweat-stained army shirt was wielding a broom in the foyer. When he came to the outer step and Hayden saw the carpet slippers on the bare feet he asked if the man was the superintendent and the fellow said he was.

"Only that ain't the word for it down here, mister," he added. "Here, in this building anyway, I'm the janitor."

Hayden knew the police had been here and that the man probably was aware of what had happened to Adler. With little hope that he could find anything useful in Adler's apartment, he nevertheless wanted to take a look. Now he took a ten-dollar bill from his cash reserve and folded it, so that the janitor could see it.

"Sam Adler lived here, didn't he?"

"That's right. In 2-B." The man stepped out on the sidewalk and jabbed a thumb upward at the right-hand corner of the building. "But you ain't about to find him. He got himself killed a couple of days ago up North."

"I'd like to take a look at his apartment anyway."

The man examined him with half-closed eyes, his hands capping the top of the broom handle and his chin propped on his hands.

"The cops already shook it down pretty good. You ain't another one, are you?"

Hayden shook his head and tried to look bored. "Insurance," he said, accepting the first thought that came to him. "Just wanted to check some things." He crackled the ten-dollar bill suggestively between his thumb and index finger. "You got a key?"

The gesture got the man's attention. A dirty-nailed hand reached out to snatch the bill and palm it.

"Help yourself," he said and then he laughed, a cackling triumphant sound. "Door ain't locked."

It was nearly dark on the sidewalk now and it was even darker inside until Hayden came in range of the electric ceiling light on the second-floor landing. When he reached it he doubled back toward the front of the building and came to this door on the left. Habit made him knock and he paused for several seconds until he realized the gesture had been unnecessary.

He opened the door and left it that way, so that the reflected light from the hall gave him a look at the shadowy interior. When he saw the lamp on the table directly ahead, he reached for it, and the instant he turned the switch he was aware of some faint warmth under the shade.

The knowledge that someone was here, or had been a few minutes earlier, stirred up a quick excitement and put new pressure on his nerve ends. A slow inspection of the disordered living room gave him the impression that this was a fitting habitat for the picture his mind had conjured up of Sam Adler. Even when new, the furniture could have had neither charm nor distinction, but after his first glance his interest centered on the suitcase which lay on the floor opposite the oblong table where he stood.

He could see that the catches had not been fastened and wondered why. Then, his glance noting the empty but darkened inner hallway, he considered the two closed doors, one apparently leading to an adjoining room, the other one just inside the hall door, which still stood open.

He went to this now, feeling some tension in his back and neck but no alarm. As he closed it he remembered a phrase he had used as a kid: "Come out, come out, wherever you are." This was what he had in mind now but he phrased it differently.

"Come on out," he called, his voice sounding loud in the quiet room. "Come on," he said again, a little surprised at his new-found boldness. "I don't want to have to drag you."

The second command brought results. He heard a doorknob turn, the click of a latch. As he glanced around, a door opened and a woman emerged from the adjoining bedroom. She did not advance but stood in the opening, and in those first moments she seemed enough like Doris Lamar to be her sister.

The tinted blond hair looked much the same and so did her over-all appearance. From that distance, and in the half-light of the room, the resemblance seemed remarkable, but it was, he knew at once, only an impression and a product of his imagination. For this woman was a little older, a little thinner, a little shabbier somehow. The eyes seemed dark and suspicious in the pointed face, and now when she spoke her voice sounded harsh and direct.

"Who are you?"

"I was about to ask the same question," Hayden said. "If you have to have a name, John will do."

"What do you want?"

"I came to have a look around. How about you?"

"I've got a right to be here."

"You wouldn't be Mrs. Adler, would you?"

"No, I'm not Mrs. Adler," she said, biting off the words. "But I stayed here sometimes. Sam was away a lot. He let me use the place."

She came slowly forward then in a nondescript blue print dress, apparently no longer worried about him, and now, in the circle of the light, he knew that she had never been as attractive as Doris Lamar. There may have been at one time a superficial prettiness about her face, but it looked tired, worn, and discouraged now, the dark brown eyes mirroring disillusionment and defeat.

"The name is Flo," she said flatly. "You a friend of Sam's?" she added with some suspicion.

"No," Hayden said, "but I know what happened to him."

"So do I. The cops rousted me around a bit yesterday and I know Sam's not coming back."

"Is that why you were packing the suitcase?"

"Why shouldn't I? I've got some things here. So did Sam. If I don't take 'em, who will? The rent's paid till the first of the month and the janitor said I could stay here and why not?"

Hayden was about to agree with her but he had no chance. Even as he opened his mouth he saw her glance dart beyond him and then widen instantly. He understood at once that she was staring at the hall door, and something in her manner so disturbed him that he spun quickly to face the new threat she had seen.

It may have been the abrupt violence of his move that brought the reaction from the man who had so silently opened the door and stood upon the threshold. It may have been a simple act of self-defense that had been motivated by some new suspicion. Whatever the reason, the man's hand had moved as Hayden completed his turn, and now he found himself staring into the muzzle of a revolver that looked very large and very threatening. Only when he could bring his eyes up to inspect the tanned, good-looking face did recognition come to him; only then did he understand that he had found Ted Corbin at last.

CHAPTER 14

IN THOSE FIRST SILENT seconds when no one moved and no one could find anything to say, Hayden offered silent thanks for the luck, coincidence, or good fortune that had finally paid off for his gamble and his persistence. He did not know what would happen now, but he felt a confidence that had not been there before, and he understood at once why Marion had been attracted to Corbin.

He seemed now to realize that Hayden presented no great threat and he let the gun swing down. He reached behind him to close the door, a big man, standing a good six feet two and weighing two-twenty or so, most of it bone and muscle. His blond hair was thick and worn fairly short, his mouth was wide, the jaw solidly shaped. His nose was a little off line, as though bent permanently in some football combat long ago, but the eyes were blue and well spaced and the tan gave him a look of strength and vitality. Waiting there in slacks, sport shirt, and flannel jacket, he had a puzzled look until Hayden spoke.

"Hello, Corbin."

The big man did not do very well with the question. The eyes widened slowly and the mouth opened. For five seconds he simply stared and beneath the tan the muscles were suddenly slack. Then recovery came and he had himself in hand. The eyes wrinkled at the corners as a slow smile that had little warmth but was effective because of his white and even teeth took over.

"Corbin?" he said as though finding the word unfamiliar. "Un-unh. Cannon's the name," he added, a trace of southern accent coming through. "Ted Cannon."

"Marion used to have a good picture of you," Hayden said. "I saw it many times."

"Marion?" The word was touched with wonderment. "Marion?" he said again, and then, as the message got through, acceptance came. "Oh, I see. And who the hell are you?"

"Her husband. I'm John Hayden."

Corbin's shoulders seemed to sag beneath the jacket as he took a labored breath. As though becoming aware of the gun in his hand, he tucked it somewhere inside his waistband. He seemed to be searching for words, but Flo, who had been taking all this with increasing annoyance, spoke first.

"What is this?" she demanded querulously. "If you're going to have a conference take it outside, will you?"

Corbin looked at her curiously. He looked at Hayden.

"Who's this?"

"I'll tell you who I am," Flo said and proceeded to do so.

Corbin's smile came back, crooked now but tolerant. "So you're picking up the pieces, hunh?"

"Who's got a better right? Why don't you two beat it and get off my back?"

"We will," Hayden said, "if you'll tell us about Adler."

"Why should I?"

"I don't know if the police know you're cleaning out the place," he added, "but we could ask them."

She seemed about to argue but thought better of it. "All right." She sat down, her tired face sullen. "What do you want to know?"

"You were Sam's girl friend—"

"One of them."

"So you must have some idea why he went North."

"He said he had a deal on."

"When did he first say so?"

"I don't know. Maybe a month ago. I didn't think much about it at first. He always had some kind of a deal cooking but nothing much ever happened."

"When did he leave?"

"Saturday. He said he'd be back by the end of this week. He wouldn't give any details. He said he was going to make a big score and when he collected we were going to Florida for a while."

Hayden considered the statement and found it acceptable. It was the same line Adler had given to Doris Lamar, apparently with some success.

"He didn't tell you how he was going to make that score?"

"No."

He glanced at Corbin, who had been watching the woman, a sardonic expression working in his blue eyes.

"I guess you knew Adler."

Corbin nodded. "I knew him."

"And what happened to him?"

"There were a couple of paragraphs in the paper."

"I think we have some talking to do."

"About what?"

Hayden paused reflectively, his mind working smoothly. He was ready to accept Flo's presence here for what it was, and he doubted if she could be of any help to him now. What happened here, or what she took from the apartment, was no concern of his.

"About why you're here, what you expected to find. I have an idea about that and I can tell you about the deal Adler had in mind when he came to Connecticut."

"What makes you think I'd be interested?"

"You'd better be."

"Yeah? Why?"

"The police are looking for you and so are the insurance people; maybe even the FBI." That the police were probably looking for him too was something that Corbin could not yet know, and Hayden continued with confidence: "All I have to do to prove it is pick up the telephone. I think my way is better. Is there a bar around where we can get a drink while I make a proposition?"

"I could use a drink, but we don't have bars in this state," Corbin said, "not the way you think of them. You can get a drink at most hotels and some restaurants. But you sit down, like in a cocktail lounge, and somebody mixes your drink, using a miniature bottle like you get in Pullman cars. Otherwise you get your own bottle at a State Store and drink it at home. Where are you staying?"

Hayden told him and Corbin said: "We've got to eat anyway and the food's okay there. We'll get our drink at the same place.... You through here?"

Hayden said that he was. He had come here like a man grabbing at straws in the hope of learning something that would help him. Now that he had found his man, he had no further interest in this apartment or the woman who called herself Flo. There was much he had to know about Corbin, but that, he felt, would come if he played his cards right.

"Yes," he said. "I've had enough of this."

"Me too," Corbin said and glanced at the woman. "Take it easy, doll."

"Oh, sure." The woman opened the suitcase and began to rearrange the things she had collected. "If it's all right with you let's forget we ever saw each other." She turned her weary, disillusioned eyes to Hayden. "That goes for you too, Buster."

———◦———

When they had settled in a dimly lighted corner of the motel lounge with drinks before them, Corbin said: "How's Marion? How long have you two been married?"

"Fourteen months," Hayden said, "and right now she's four months pregnant. That should give you some idea how she felt when we found out you were probably still alive."

"Yeah." Corbin lit a cigarette and frowned at it, his expression genuinely concerned. "I never thought it could happen. How did you find out? Adler?"

"You knew him. You had to know him, otherwise you wouldn't have come to his place. What were you looking for?"

"I don't know exactly. I've been away. I saw this piece in the paper. I thought I'd take a look at the apartment, just in case."

"Maybe you were looking for these."

Hayden took out the photographs he had originally taken from Adler's wallet and spread them on the table. It seemed to him then that Corbin knew a lot about Adler, just as Adler must have known much about Corbin. How all this had come about was something he hoped to find out in time, but it could wait. He indicated the two pictures.

"He came to Marion with these. He asked for twenty thousand dollars."

Corbin looked at the pictures, the frown still there, the concern still showing in the tanned face. "The miserable little bastard," he said softly and then listened as Hayden explained why he had the enlargement made of the insignia on the coveralls, and how he had come finally to the filling station in Fairview.

"The fellow I talked with—"

"That was Joe Quinn."

"—gave you a lot of protection. A real suspicious character."

Corbin grunted softly. "The natives around here don't always open up with Yankees, especially curious ones.... Who killed Adler?"

"Did you know he was coming to Connecticut to collect on what he knew?"

For the first time there was a moment of hesitancy in Corbin's manner. His blue gaze, which until that instant had been direct, slid to the glass in his hand and he drained it before he replied.

"No." He put the glass down. "The papers said he was stabbed."

"In the back," Hayden said, "with a kitchen knife."

"The police haven't made any arrests?"

"Not yet."

"What do they think?"

"They think maybe I did it, maybe even Marion."

"You mean they know about those pictures of me? How?"

"The Connecticut police found a Conti Street address for Adler. The Mobile people got right on it. They found the two prints and two negatives. They sent the snapshot of you up by plane and they were checking the fingerprints with Washington when I left."

"What do you want with me?"

"I want you to come back."

"With you?"

"Yes."

Apparently the thought had not occurred to Corbin. He looked at Hayden with one eye, and then with both. The grin that came to warp his mouth was tight and twisted.

"Why?"

"Because it's going to be a lot easier that way."

"For whom?"

"For everybody." Hayden put his elbows on the table and leaned on them. When he continued, his tone was direct and forceful. "The police are probably looking for me too," he said. "If you go back with me I can justify this trip. What difference can it make to you? If I found you, so will the police. It's just a question of time, and believe me they're looking for you. Somebody's got to get a divorce and in a hurry. Marion's worried about the baby and so am I."

"I could get a divorce in this state in no time," Corbin said. "Or Marion could duck down here and get it."

"But there's also a little matter of seventy-five thousand dollars in insurance."

"Yeah," Corbin said and this time the grin, while reluctant, was genuine. "But I didn't get it. I had amnesia. Marion collected in good faith—"

"It has to be paid back."

"I can't help you much there.... How about you?"

"I can't make it all at once." Hayden digressed to explain how the money had been used and the benefit he derived from it. "I'll have to pay it back—most of it anyway—but I'm willing to work something out with the insurance company if I can clear up the rest of this."

Corbin shrugged and pushed his chair back. "I guess maybe you've got a point," he said slowly in that faint southern accent. "I don't want to see Marion hurt. I thought I was doing her a favor in the first place two years ago. I thought I had it made.... Let's eat," he said abruptly. "We'll work something out."

CHAPTER 15

THE INTERIOR OF TED Corbin's cottage was an improvement over the jerry-built look of the exterior. The front room bore no sign of a woman's touch and the furniture had been selected with an eye to comfort rather than style. Photographs on the walls testified to the owner's interest in the outdoor life—Corbin with a dead deer, Corbin and friends with a day's bag of quail, Corbin posing proudly with a sizable tarpon—but the chairs, the couch, the television set were in good condition and the room had an over-all look of bachelor neatness.

Hayden had followed Corbin across the causeway in his rented car because, while Corbin had given the impression that he was ready to fly back and straighten out the situation he had created, Hayden wanted to stay with the big man until they were actually on the plane. Now, coming in from the kitchen with a bottle of bourbon and glasses and a pitcher of water, he sat down opposite Hayden and stretched his legs out, the ankles crossed.

"I told you I'd tell you what happened two years ago," he said, "and try to explain the series of stupid incidents that kept me from getting on the plane that night in Capitol City. It's a long story."

"I've got time," Hayden said.

"And it's in two parts. The first concerns me. The second has to do with Adler. It'll show you what a conniving little bastard he was and how he got things ready to collect on what he knew."

He waved a hand as an invitation to pour a drink but Hayden said he'd wait. Corbin nodded and took time to light a cigarette. When he had inhaled, his gaze moved to the opposite wall and a small frown began to work on the tanned, handsome face.

"I guess it starts with Marion and me," he said. "I mean the fact that our marriage hadn't worked out and was about to bust up. I don't know how much she told you about me—where I was brought up and where I went to school and what I was doing when she met me."

He paused while Hayden related the few things Marion had told him. He nodded absently.

"That's about right," he said. "I liked football and I played a couple of years of the pro game but I couldn't quite cut it. I mean, I could see I'd never be a first-string regular, but I always liked to hunt and fish, and those were things Marion had no interest in whatsoever. Oh, I guess we were in love all right when we were married, but, after six months or so, everything seemed to start going downhill and it was probably a lot more my fault than it was hers.

"I mean, we just weren't interested in the same things. It was hard to talk to each other. She liked to read; I didn't. She liked to go to the theater, sometimes to a concert. She liked music—Dixie, the classics, anything that was good. I just couldn't seem to get with that sort of stuff, but I think it was the friends we had that made things worse. A man and woman just can't get along by themselves. They have to have friends and outside contacts and mutual interests, don't they?

"My friends," he added, expecting no answer, "were basically guys like me. I knew some guys on the Giants and the Eagles, a couple in baseball. In football season I'd look them up or they'd look me up. They'd come to the apartment or maybe we'd go out somewhere for dinner. Real good guys, some of them with nice wives, but Marion simply couldn't tune in on that kind of talk. It was even worse for me. She had her friends and we'd be out with them at parties and I had a hard time finding anything to say that anybody would listen to.

"I don't mean they were snooty. They liked Marion and they wanted to like me, but about half the conversation was chitchat that didn't mean anything and was about people I didn't even know. The rest of it, the men I mean, was talk about stocks and investments and taxes and politics and golf handicaps and trips they had made." He stopped and looked at Hayden. "Does any of this make any sense?"

"It makes a lot of sense," Hayden said.

"So the marriage wasn't working out and we both knew it. We both tried too, I think. But somehow I started to drink a little more than I should and I'd get to brooding and wondering what I could do to fix things up. Instead of getting out and trying to sell, I'd duck into an afternoon movie and brood some more. So I lost a job and then another and another. I was about to lose again when I went out to Kansas City to see if I could swing one more deal.

"I was working for a paper box company at the time, and I thought maybe if I could get a big order I could hang on a while longer, not that it probably would have done any good because we were already talking about separation and divorce. Marion had started to look for a job and I guess we both understood there wasn't any future in it for us the way things were."

He stopped again and, as though just becoming aware of the bottle of whisky, reached for it. He pulled his legs in and sat up; he made two drinks, not asking Hayden if he wanted one. He passed it over silently and Hayden accepted. Corbin took a big swallow, put the glass down, and again his gaze moved away and distance grew in it.

"This was right after New Year's," he said, "and on New Year's they have all those college bowl games and I hit three out of four. I had six hundred dollars in my kick when I got the plane that day. I went out to Kansas City. I made my pitch. No dice. So I had one more chance, a job I'd heard about that was opening up for an outfit in Capitol City. So I went there. Same thing. I said what I had to say and they listened. They didn't say no but I didn't think I was going to get the job either.

"Well, this is late Friday afternoon and I'm feeling too sorry for myself to go home yet. But the next day, Saturday, they're having the play-off of the two runner-up teams in the National Football League. The Bisons are five-to-nine underdogs but I like 'em. I have this six hundred bucks, so I lay five of it on the Bisons and they win by one point in the last forty seconds. So now I've got around fifteen hundred bucks—more than I've had since I can remember—and it's late Saturday afternoon, so now we come to the trench coat."

Hayden remembered the trench coat. That coat, and what had been in its pockets, had been all-important in establishing Corbin's death, and now he put his glass aside and waited, his dark eyes somber and intent.

"I'd had that trench coat since before I married," Corbin said, "and Marion hated it. Maybe not at first, but I always wore it when I could, and I guess it got to be looking pretty disreputable. Anyway she said it was. About once a week she'd make some crack about it. Why couldn't I get a neat cloth coat like other men? She didn't say I looked like a bum but that's what she thought."

He grunted softly and an absent smile was reflected in his eyes. "I guess it did get to be pretty crummy-looking, and for some reason I remembered how she felt about it that Saturday afternoon. So I walked into this store with all that fresh money in my pocket and bought a new one.

"I didn't have too much time and the sleeves had to be lengthened about an inch but that salesman wanted the sale. I told him I couldn't wait, that I had things to do. He said he could send it to the airport but I thought of something else. I said if he'd have it wrapped up and ready, I'd have my taxi come by that way and pick it up. I told him if it wasn't ready for me by the front door there'd be no sale and he promised it would be there.... It was," he said, and took another swallow of his drink.

"So I rode out to the airport and got a quick double bourbon and water. I was feeling pretty good then and I'd never taken any flight insurance before, but I got to thinking that now that I had some real money this would be the time the damn plane would crash, so I stopped and got this policy for Marion. I'd already wired her I'd be on that flight, so I went over to the counter, handed over my suitcase and ticket."

He grunted softly again, an introspective sound. "The fellow stapled the baggage check to that part of the ticket they give you back—you know, the carbon part. The clerk handed me a landing pass and then I took off for the men's room to try on my new coat. The room was empty except for two guys who were sitting on a bench and two sadder-looking characters you never saw. One was on the small side, with an old felt hat and a topcoat on. The other fellow was nearly as tall as I am but not as big around. He wore a wrinkled suit with a sweater on underneath it but no coat.

"What I didn't know was that they were pals and were actually together. Because they weren't sitting that way. I mean, the tall guy was hunched over reading a newspaper; the little guy was sitting by himself at the other side of the room, slumped back, his hat over his eyes like he was half asleep. I probably gave him a quick look when I walked in but I never really saw his face.

"I undid the package and chucked the paper into a trash can. I tried the coat on and liked it and was about to throw the old coat on top of the wrapping paper too when I thought about this guy who didn't have a coat. I turned around and asked him if he could use it. I said it was pretty dirty but it might not be too bad once he got it cleaned and he was welcome to it if he wanted it. He did. He thanked me, and as I started out I could hear the flight being called over the loud-speaker."

He paused again, the blue eyes full of thought as his mind went back.

"But I was a little juiced by that time and feeling pretty good. I knew that the first call for a flight—and lots of times the second call—didn't mean a thing, and since I was all cleared away I decided I had time for another drink. I heard the second call but I was just mulled enough to think I had plenty of time. Anyway I finished my drink, paid the check, and started for the gate."

He took a breath and let it out slowly. He looked again at Hayden and that small smile was still there.

"I guess you know how it must have been and what happened after that."

"I guess so," Hayden said.

"It was a lot longer walk than I thought. This particular gate was way-the-hell-and-gone at the end of the corridor, and when I got there the attendant who had been checking off the passengers was just turning away.

The gate was closed. I could see the passenger ramp being wheeled away from the plane and the door was shut. Two of the motors had already started. I knew I didn't have a chance but I thought I'd try. I stuck my hand into my new coat pocket to get my boarding pass and the carbon to my ticket and my baggage check and—you guessed it—I'd forgotten to take them out of the old coat."

"Ahh—" said Hayden as he visualized the picture. "By then it was too late—"

"Hell yes. I asked the attendant if everybody was checked aboard. He said yes, and by that time I was too disgusted with myself to put up a beef. I knew it wouldn't do any good. It was my own damn fault, and I knew that skinny guy was sitting there in my seat, that he not only would get a free ride to New York but probably claim my suitcase.

"I was so damn mad I didn't even go back to the counter and tell them what had happened. I wasn't even sure I could make them believe it or prove what I said. I just stood there and watched the plane take off and then I went back to the bar, not thinking that I ought to call Marion and tell her I missed the flight. I tied on a pretty good one for the next hour or so and then I walked out of the terminal and across the road to this motel, paid for a room, and went to bed to sleep it off."

He stood up, the tanned face grave as remembered thoughts came back to haunt him.

"If I'd hung around the airport a few more minutes I'd have known about the crash. But I didn't. I got the word from a newspaper I bought when I went into the motel restaurant for breakfast the next morning, and I guess for a while after that I was in a state of shock. I still wake up scared some nights when I think of it. You can't believe what a thing like that can do to you."

He walked the length of the room and came back. "I should have been dead but I wasn't. I kept thinking of that plane and how I'd seen it take off and the crazy twist of luck that kept me off it. I couldn't get it out of my mind. I read my name on the list of victims. I knew that Marion already had the word that she was a widow."

He stopped pacing to look at Hayden. "The idea that there was my chance to make the break that was long overdue didn't come all at once. It grew a thought at a time as that feeling of shock and unreality began to wear off. I didn't have any plan then. I only knew that here was a chance I'd never get again to start a new life not only for myself but for Marion. There was no love for us any more, no future together. She wouldn't grieve much. She'd already had the shock of knowing I was gone for good, and now she'd have seventy-five thousand bucks, more than I could ever have left her any other way."

He paused again and said in slow accents: "Only one guy on earth besides myself knew that I hadn't gone down with that plane. The little guy in the men's room."

"Adler."

"Right. I thought about him before the day was out, but in my mind he was only some itinerant bum, and the odds that he could foul up my scheme were a million to one." He stepped to an open doorway, reached in, and snapped on a light. "But that's the second part of my story and it can wait."

He disappeared inside the room and Hayden could see enough of the interior to know that this was a bedroom. Presently he heard a telephone being dialed and then Corbin's voice.

"Connie? I'm coming over for a few minutes.... Yeah.... No, I can't tonight but I have to see you. Yeah, right away."

He came back to the living room and headed for the outside door.

"I told you I'd probably go back with you," he said. "You can count on it. Not just for you and Marion either."

"For Connie?" Hayden said, hazarding a guess.

"Yeah." The grin came slowly, the teeth white against the tanned muscular face. "I guess I've been kidding myself too long.... I'll be back in a half hour," he added. "Stick around."

CHAPTER 16

JOHN HAYDEN REMAINED IN his chair for several minutes after the door closed, his drink forgotten and his mind evaluating the story he had heard. Even in retrospect he could not quarrel with it. It held, somehow, a ring of truth, and he found he could accept the incredible twist of fate that had saved Corbin's life on that January night more than two years ago. There was much he did not understand about what had happened since that time, but even now he found it difficult to blame Corbin for what he had done.

He had thought earlier that he understood Marion's original attraction to the man. He was of the same opinion now. For while Corbin was obviously no mental giant, he had, in addition to his good looks, a charm that was forthright and basically friendly. The motives which influenced his disappearance were simple and uncomplicated. He was willing now to face the music without fuss and, on balance, Hayden could not help but like him. This thought helped to bolster his own confidence, and as his mind went on, he rose and started aimlessly about the room.

The light was still on in the adjoining bedroom and he stopped in the doorway to glance inside. That was how he happened to see the suitcase which stood at the foot of the double bed. There was nothing unusual about the case. It was a brown canvas-covered bag, man-sized, lightweight, and medium-priced by the look of it. If he had not so recently made a flight from New York he might not have wondered about the baggage tag which still hung from the handle.

He knew it was the passenger's half of the baggage check that the attendant had not bothered to remove when the suitcase was reclaimed. He also recalled that Corbin had been away. The suspicious character in the filling station had said something about Corbin and a trip North. This knowledge prompted Hayden to move inside and step closer to the suitcase, but it was simple curiosity rather than suspicion that made him examine the tag.

Not understanding yet the implications of his discovery, he simply read the large block letters imprinted on the thin white cardboard. The abbreviations told him at once that this suitcase had been checked from New York to Mobile.

The top numbers meant nothing but there was a flight number that did. This had been written in with a blue crayon, and as he repeated the number aloud he knew that this was the same flight he had taken that morning.

He straightened slowly, his angular face twisting absently and his dark gaze puzzled. He stood that way for long seconds, knowing that Corbin must have been in New York recently. Then, stooping again, he flipped the tag over and saw the date that had been stamped there. Only then did he realize that Corbin had taken the same flight South that he had, but exactly twenty-four hours earlier.

Why?

That is what he asked himself as he grappled with his new-found information. He let his breath out slowly, not knowing that he had been holding it. He considered the days of the week and a curious feeling of tension began to work on him as he realized that Corbin had probably been in New York the night Sam Adler was killed. The assumption was sound but it was still only an assumption. Corbin could have been in New York for any number of reasons. But when had he arrived? How long had he stayed and what—?

The sound of the car moving in from the street to park alongside the porch jerked his thoughts back to the moment, and his immediate reaction was swift and impulsive. Not really thinking, not even sure what prompted the move, he quickly loosened the cord that held the tag. When he had a loop he slipped the piece of cardboard through the opening and it came free in his hand. Even as he straightened again a new thought came to disturb him but he dismissed it arbitrarily. Maybe Corbin would miss that tag and maybe not, but it was too late now for doubts, and he was back in the living room, the tag safely in his pocket, when the door opened.

The big man's grin seemed genuine as he entered the room, and there was no indecision in his manner as he started for the bedroom, stopping only long enough to pick up his glass and the whisky bottle.

"Bring your glass," he said. "Water if you want it. I'd better start packing."

Hayden followed him to the door, a nervousness assailing him as Corbin picked up the suitcase and tossed it on the bed. He watched the big man pour a small drink and toss it off, saw him put the glass aside and open the suitcase. When he turned to pull out a drawer in the chest, Hayden gave a small and silent sigh of relief, emptied his own glass, and started to relax.

"You were going to tell me about Adler," he said. "And why you came to Mobile."

"Yeah," Corbin said, "and the last part is easy. Once I finally decided to make the break I thought of it right off and for three reasons: I didn't know anybody here and that meant nobody would know me, I liked the country, and it was far, far away from New York."

"You'd been here before?"

"One summer while I was in college I worked for a while on the docks. I liked to hunt and fish even then, and this country gives you both. Deer, quail, dove, turkey; even ducks if you want to go west a hundred miles."

He stopped to consider the things he had already packed and when he continued there was a noticeable enthusiasm in his voice.

"As for fish, you name it, we've got it. I don't mean you can just toss out a line and get the limit any time you want to, but if you like to fish this is the place. Fresh water, salt water. Lakes and rivers, the Bay, Mississippi Sound, the Gulf. I'll never forget a trip I took that summer with four guys from the docks. We chartered a boat at Bayou La Batre. We were out three days and we had fishing that was fishing.

"Anyway," he added, as though aware that he was digressing, "I decided this was the place for me. I mean, after I finally decided to run and that took a while. I remember I went from the motel over to the air terminal and found out what I could about the crash. I was still sort of in shock and I bought myself a bottle in a liquor store there and I sucked on it from time to time. Maybe what I got out of that bottle gave me the courage I needed. I got a bus into town and I had this fifteen hundred bucks in my pocket and I knew that was all I was going to have until I got down here and got a job. I found out I could get a bus that afternoon that would take me here by way of New Orleans, so I got myself a seat. But, what the hell, you don't want details."

He again glanced about the room to see if he had forgotten anything.

"I picked the name Cannon—don't ask me why—and I used it that afternoon. I've been using it ever since. I got a room in a small hotel and started looking for work. I couldn't use my Social Security card or driver's license or anything like that, so when I got a chance to go to work for this filling station at sixty bucks a week I told the guy I never had had a Social Security card. I told him I'd always worked on a farm, but he needed help and he wasn't too fussy. I got a new card and eventually a new driver's license.

"After I'd been around awhile," he said, "I got to like Fairview and I finally got the job with Quinn. I hung onto my dough, and when the next fall came around I did pretty good betting on the football games again. I rented this place and got me a small boat, and before long I found out that Quinn had a very attractive kid sister."

"Connie?" Hayden asked.

"Connie," Corbin said, and the smile in his eyes told Hayden how the big man felt about the girl. "Quinn and I got along and I saved my dough and now

I've got a third interest in that filling station. I thought I was all set. I had it made. The past was kicked and then that son-of-a-bitch Adler turned up."

"He must have known all the time," Hayden said, having only a vague idea of how such a thing could happen but understanding that this was so.

"Hell yes, he knew." Corbin stopped his packing and the blue eyes were suddenly cold and resentful. "He started snooping and figuring that first day. He didn't have any angle then, but he could tell from what I did that I had one. He wouldn't let it go. He couldn't figure out why I acted the way I did and it bothered him. He had to find out what I was after and if there was anything in it for him. He said it was curiosity at first."

"You got the story out of him?"

"I got it. He'd have made a damn good detective," he added bitterly, "especially a dishonest one."

"He saw his pal get on the plane," Hayden said.

"Sure. But what you have to understand, the thing that gave Adler a chance to follow up was that I didn't know these two were together. How could I? I told you I was a little juiced when I walked into that men's room. I'm interested in trying on a new coat and getting out of there. I notice a little guy slumped in the corner, his hat half over his eyes like he's trying to sleep. I see this other guy at the opposite end of the room, reading a newspaper that looked like it had been picked out of a trash can. This is the guy I see. This is the fellow I gave the trench coat to."

"When he found the ticket and your boarding pass in the pocket," Hayden said, "he decided to take a chance on using them and see if he could get away with it."

"Right.... They were horse players," Corbin said, "and they were trying to get to Florida or New Orleans, but they had only enough dough between them to get one of them down there. They were hanging around trying to keep warm and waiting for something to happen. The minute they realized they had a chance to get my seat they pooled their cash and Adler took it, the other guy figuring if he can make New York he's got friends who can give him a hand.

"And because I have to have a couple more drinks," he added savagely, "and I'm stupid enough to think maybe the plane will wait for me, they pulled it off. Adler keeps an eye on me, at first to see if I'm going back to the airline counter to make a beef and after that just because he's got that kind of curious, conniving mind. He follows me over to the motel and knows that I register and go to my room. He comes back to the terminal building and a few minutes later he gets word of the crash. He's got nowhere to go and nothing to do so he hangs around. All he knows then is that his pal got a bad break and that I'm a very lucky guy."

He took a breath and said: "He's still there the next morning when I come in. He knows the score. He wonders what I'm going to do. He sees me get the pint from the liquor store, and he can't figure out why I should be acting like that, so when I get a bus back to town, he's on it. By the time I get to the bus terminal in town I know what I'm going to do. I buy a ticket to Mobile in the name of Ted Cannon, and since he's going South anyway he decides to come along."

"You didn't recognize him?" Hayden asked.

"I didn't know he was alive," Corbin said. "To me he's a little guy—he's got dark glasses on now—I've never seen before. We even have a little conversation on that trip because by now he knows I'm doing a run-out and he's beginning to smell a payoff somewhere. He goes to the same cheap hotel I do, and a couple days later when I get a job he finds out where I got it. After that I don't see him again until a couple of months ago when he turns up at the filling station."

Hayden was ready to accept this much. He also knew that Corbin knew a great deal about Sam Adler and somewhere in his mind a small seed of suspicion began to put out shoots.

"But how could he know about Marion?" he asked.

"How could he miss with a mind like his? He read the papers, just like I did. It was all there if you wanted it—names and addresses of victims, those that had been identified, those that weren't. Because they didn't know what caused the crash for a while, the insurance angle came out too. Adler not only knew my New York City address but he knew that Marion was going to collect seventy-five thousand dollars. That was all he needed to get the idea that maybe someday there'd be some dough in it for him."

He closed the top of the suitcase and said: "I don't mean he made a career out of this during the next two years, but he always had it in the back of his mind. And remember he was a horse player. New Orleans, Hollywood, Miami in the winter; Aqueduct, Belmont, Narragansett, Suffolk Downs in the summer. He may have had a little help in New York—he didn't say—to keep a check on what Marion did. On one trip he found out she got married. He found out where you lived. He never forgot that she had collected seventy-five thousand dollars and he eventually found out that you had your own business and were doing pretty well in it. When he got ready he made his first move."

"How?"

"He drove into the filling station one day," Corbin said. "I knew I'd seen him somewhere but I didn't remember him. I thought he was just another customer I'd seen before. He took that snapshot of me without me knowing it. While I was working on the car I must have put my hand on the hood because later he got somebody to lift those fingerprints and photograph them. I didn't know anything about it until he showed up one evening and made his pitch."

"Here?"

"Right in that other room. He showed me the two snapshots. He told me when he'd taken them and why. He told me the story and it didn't make any difference whether I believed him or not; the point was he knew what had happened. He knew I was Ted Corbin. He knew about the insurance and he knew about Marion."

He yanked the suitcase from the bed with a quick and angry movement. He set it on the floor and when he turned there were hard bright glints in the narrowed blue eyes.

"I told you he'd been snooping," he said, "and not just about Marion and you. Somehow he knew I had an interest in the gas station. He knew about my car and my boat and Connie. He had to guess about one thing—that we planned to get married—but he was right."

"How much did he want?"

"Five thousand. He said he'd take twenty-five hundred now and I could get the other twenty-five hundred up in six months or whenever I could.... I should have killed him then," he said savagely. "I'd have been acquitted in this county. He was carrying a gun and I could have sworn that he threatened me."

Hayden considered the statement in the brief silence that followed. He wondered about the phrasing of certain words but he did not dwell on them because he had to know the rest of it.

"What *did* you do?"

Corbin shrugged. He gestured emptily with one brown hand. His gaze seemed distant and withdrawn and when he spoke the savagery had gone from his tone.

"I guess I didn't play it very smart," he said. "I was too burned right then to realize that he could hit you and Marion without ever coming directly to me again. I started for him and knocked him down and threw him out. I threw the gun out after him. I told him if I ever saw him again or even heard from him he'd wind up in the Bay with an anchor around his neck."

He took a slow breath and the look in his eyes suggested that he was seeing again the scene he had described. "I meant it," he added with quiet emphasis, "and Adler knew I meant it—"

His head jerked around as the sound of the telephone punctuated his sentence. It was loud and startling, that sound, its unexpectedness holding both men immobile until it rang again. This time Corbin strode over and swept the instrument off its rack.

"Yeah?" He listened then and Hayden could see the quick frown and the growing uncertainty in the blue eyes. "You sure?... Yeah.... Right.... Thanks, pal, I'll be in touch when I can."

He hung up and reached for the suitcase in the same continuous movement. The frown was still there on the tanned good-looking face but the eyes were thoughtful now and there was a thin, mirthless smile on the mouth.

"My partner," he said. "A Mobile cop, a sheriff's deputy, and an insurance man are looking for me. Let's go."

Hayden had to move fast to get out of Corbin's way and then they were crossing the living room and turning out lights and coming finally to the screened porch. As they went down the steps Hayden said:

"How much time have we got?"

"Enough. Quinn had to give them an address, so he told them I lived on North Oak Street. This is South. Follow me in your car," he said.

Hayden did not argue. He tailed Corbin's sedan until Corbin parked it out behind the filling station, approaching from the side street. Corbin transferred his suitcase to the back seat of Hayden's rented car and climbed in beside him. He said if the word was out he might be picked up in his own car, but with a rented car there should be no trouble.

CHAPTER 17

TED CORBIN MADE A good suggestion as they came out of the tunnel into downtown Mobile. The half-hour drive from Fairview had been uneventful and silent, but now Corbin stirred in his corner of the seat and Hayden could feel the shadowed gaze inspecting him.

"Did you rent this car in your own name?"

"I had to," Hayden said. "Had to use my credit card."

"Well, we know they're looking for me. From what you say there could be a fugitive warrant out for you."

"There probably is."

"I don't know about flights out of here at this time of night. I do know that an airport is one of the first places a cop would check, and now that I've decided to go back I'd rather make the trip with you than with the law."

"What have you got in mind?"

"New Orleans. They've probably got twenty times as many flights a day out of there as they have out of here and it's a hell of a lot bigger terminal. We can stop and pick up your bag at the motel and keep moving."

"How far?"

"Maybe three hours."

"Okay," Hayden said, "just keep me on the right road."

"Stay on 90—all the way."

At the motel Hayden did not bother to turn off the motor while he went to his room and got his hat and coat and bag he had not yet unpacked. When he started up again, Corbin settled back in his seat and Hayden gave his attention to the traffic lights on Government Street. He took no chances, then or later, and with the city behind him and the divided highway joining finally to make a two-way road, he got comfortable and settled down to his work. The highway signs told him that the state speed laws were sixty miles per hour in daylight and fifty at night, so he split the difference.

For a while the countryside was as he remembered it from his morning drive from the airport except that it was flatter here and more level. The headlights picked out oaks and pines, with here and there a pecan orchard.

Later there was a marshy area for a few miles and presently a sign announced the city limits of Pascagoula. He took care going through the town. He had to stop for a toll bridge which carried them across a wide inlet or river, and then they rode inland again until they came to Ocean Springs. Here a long bridge carried them over a wide arm of Mississippi Sound, and then he was again watching the traffic lights as they went through Biloxi.

For the next thirty miles or so the scene was unchanging. Through Gulfport, Long Beach, and Pass Christian the divided road was straight, the scene unvarying. On the left the beach was broad and gently sloping; on the right, and stretching mile after mile as one town gave way to another, the highway was bordered by homes and spacious lawns, with only an occasional motel or restaurant or filling station to break the residential continuity.

The beach ended in another toll bridge, and Corbin, who had been dozing for the past hour, sat up and produced a quarter to make the payment. Beyond the bridge was the town of Bay St. Louis, and Corbin announced that in another twenty miles they would be in Louisiana. It was some distance beyond—Hayden was never quite sure just where they were—when the highway patrol car sped up behind them.

It happened suddenly and without warning. Hayden had been watching the speedometer regularly, with an eye for the rear-view mirror from time to time, but the patrol car was coming so fast that it was almost on top of them before he saw the flashing red light and heard the first wail of the siren.

His first reaction was one of sudden alarm and his foot eased instinctively on the accelerator. There was guilt and despair in his thoughts too until he saw that the speedometer said sixty, and then he could only wait, the sweat breaking out on him and his voice sinking as he said:

"Oh-oh."

"What's the matter?" Corbin said, and then he too heard the siren. "A cop?" he said. "Oh, Jesus!"

"What's the speed limit?"

"Sixty, I guess."

"That's all I'm doing."

"Hold it that way. If we get picked up now were dead."

The driver behind touched the siren again briefly as Corbin finished. The lights were huge now in the rear-view mirror, so close that Hayden had to concentrate to keep a steady course. An instant later there was a quick *wssshhing* sound and then there was nothing but the fading throb of the sedan's motor and twin taillights that were quickly reduced to pinpoints before a slight curve blotted them from sight.

Hayden felt his heartbeat start to slow down and the back of his throat was dry. He swallowed, hearing Corbin's soft curse. He let out his breath and made an effort to steady his nerves, a new exultancy working on him now that they were safe.

"What the hell was that?" he asked. "The guy must have been going ninety."

"I don't know," Corbin said. "All I know is I'm glad he kept going."

The road had been straight for a long time and they had gone over three small concrete bridges spaced two or three miles apart. Now, coming around the curve, they saw in the distance the larger bridge. Beyond it were flares, and as they drew close Hayden saw that it was a swing bridge with three spans. He would have slowed down here anyway, but the flares in the distance made him even more cautious. He was doing no more than thirty when he saw the uniformed man with a flashlight making sweeping gestures that ordered him to keep to the left.

By that time he saw the car on its side in the ditch and the white-painted wrecker. There were two highway patrol cars parked on the shoulder; another car with its front end bashed in had slewed around perpendicular to the road.

"So that's why he was in such a hurry," Corbin said with unmistakable relief. "Keep going."

"I am," Hayden said and was very careful indeed until the lights in the rear-view mirror were gone. As he pulled his speed back up to sixty he said: "Whew! That guy scared hell out of me. How much farther?"

"Maybe thirty miles," Corbin said, "all of it easy. It just goes to show what a guilty conscience can do to a guy."

The highway cut flatly through lowlands and marshes now, with water showing here and there in the marginal area outside the bright beam of the headlights. Cheap cottages and fishing camps on stilts flanked the road with increasing frequency, and once Corbin pointed to a finger of water on the right and said it was part of Lake Pontchartrain. Then they were moving into the outskirts of the city, and Corbin, wide awake since the brush with the highway patrol, gave Hayden directions until they came finally to Moisant International Airport, with its spacious and modern terminal building.

"What do you want to do?" he said as Hayden moved past the approaches and found a parking place.

"Find out when's the best time to get out of here."

"What about the car?"

"I don't want to turn it over to the agent here, not while there's a chance they might already be looking for us. I can leave it parked anywhere around here and phone the office just before we take off. That way they can pick it up when they get around to it and bill me for the difference."

He paused to light a cigarette. "I don't even want to drive it up to the loading areas now. Too much light.... Why don't you stay here and keep an eye on our bags until I can check things and find out what the score is?"

Corbin accepted the suggestion and Hayden started off, picking his way through parked cars and coming to the lighted entrance where an overhead clock told him it was five minutes of two. A policeman, who was talking with a taxi driver, gave him no more than a passing glance as he went on into the main waiting room, which seemed strangely quiet and empty at this hour.

He slowed down here to inspect the unfamiliar area, noting signs and directional arrows as he tried to orient himself. There was a little movement on the floor, but mostly people huddled on benches in couples and family groups, silent, sleepy-eyed, and half-comatose as they waited for early-morning departures or friends who were coming in on flights from South and Central American countries that terminated here. No one paid him any attention as he continued on his way, and he was grateful for this when he came finally to the information counter.

What he learned from the lone attendant was not encouraging; neither was it unexpected. There would be no more flights to New York until morning. The first and best of these left at nine o'clock, but to find out about space he had to continue on to the airline counter, where a clerk, who had been working on a carton of coffee, put it aside long enough to give him his attention. He consulted his charts when Hayden asked his question and shook his head.

"Sorry, sir," he said. "That flight is sold out. We already have two stand-bys and I'd be glad to add your name if you would like to take a chance on some cancellations."

"What's my next-best bet?"

"We have a conventional flight at nine-twenty that makes two stops and puts you into Newark." He hesitated in order to consult another sheet. "Also one at nine-forty with one stop that terminates at Idlewild."

"Which one gets there first?"

"The nine-forty flight."

"Have you got two seats?"

"Yes, we have."

"Can I pay for them in the morning?"

"Yes, but they must be picked up an hour before takeoff." He picked up a pencil. "The names?"

"J. Hastings and T. Cannon."

Hayden thanked him, and as he turned away and his mind moved on, a thought which had been submerged in his consciousness suddenly demanded attention. Once considered, it took on a new urgency, and he walked to the newsstand near the main entrance and bought a pack of cigarettes, offering a five-dollar bill and asking for as many quarters as the clerk could spare.

For he knew now that he had to talk to Marion. He had to know how she was and what had happened; he had to tell her about Corbin. It was, he knew, a hell of an hour for a man to call his wife, especially a pregnant one—the difference in time meant that it was after three o'clock in Connecticut—but he had to let her know that things were going to be all right. He wanted to do it at once, but the thought of Corbin took him through the doors and across the parking area. He saw again the sign of the Hilton Motel he had noticed earlier and decided this would be the place to spend the night....

The thought dissolved as he came to a stop beside the sedan. Without actually moving he could feel his nerves recoil as he glanced quickly about and the first thrust of panic hit him. He knew then that he had the right car, just as he knew both seats were empty. Not understanding this, not daring to speculate, he stood where he was, shocked and incredulous, and this was long enough for the seed of suspicion he had felt earlier to send out new roots. He started to curse as the anger grew swiftly inside him, but even as he felt the impact of his discovery he heard the soft whistle that came from one side.

He spun about at the sound, peering into the shadows until he found the pale outline of a face. It took shape as Corbin moved down from behind another car, and suddenly he felt all weak inside as relief provided a swift and certain antidote to his fears. When he was sure he expelled his breath and his voice was rough and uneven.

"What the hell have you been doing?"

"Ducking a cop," Corbin said calmly. "Just to make sure." He pointed. "I saw him start down the line of cars, heading this way. I thought he was casing them. I didn't want to take a chance. I got out and ducked."

Hayden took another breath as he regained his composure. "What happened?"

"Nothing. I guess he was looking for his own car. He walked on by just before you came, got into this Ford, and drove off.... What did you find out?"

Hayden told him, and while the suspicion that had become rooted in his mind still remained, he could find no fault with Corbin's defensive measures. It was the same way with him. Until the last couple of days the law and its enforcers had been necessary adjuncts to society, designed to keep people in line. His own experience had been limited to a warning for a traffic violation. Now he not only was a prime suspect in a murder case but he had been forced to consider such things as bigamy and fraud. It was no wonder that he felt continually jumpy and on edge, and he was a little amazed that he could still carry on and do the things that had to be done. Even Corbin, whose character suggested that he was not an unduly imaginative man, felt the pressure, but now it was Hayden who had to do the thinking and take charge. He was at once aware of this as the big man said:

"Do we check in at that motel?"

"We can't sit up all night in the terminal."

"That's what I mean. Do you want to drive over there and leave the car?"

"We've got this far with it," Hayden said. "Let's leave it right here." He glanced over at the loading area and saw the three taxis parked there. "Get your bag and take a cab," he said. "Register for both of us. I'm traveling as John Hastings—and tell the clerk I'll be along in a few minutes."

Corbin did not argue. He pulled his suitcase off the back seat and started through the cars without a word. Hayden stayed where he was until he saw the other get into the taxi and drive off; then he got his own things, rolled up the windows, and put the ignition key over the sun visor, reminding himself that he must telephone the rental company before he boarded the plane in the morning.

It was cool enough now to wear the topcoat, and when he had put on his hat, he walked over to the lead taxi and put his bag in the back. He told the driver to put down his flag and wait while he made a phone call, and then he was inside and stepping into the booth. He knew that it was possible that his own telephone might be tapped, but he intended to give away nothing that would help locate him. All the odds were in his favor now. He kept the thought in mind as he deposited a coin and gave the local operator his home number.

He heard the number being relayed to a second operator, apparently in New York, and with it came a request for payment. He listened to the *bong* of the quarters as they registered, the more metallic sounds of the smaller coins as he made the exact change. Then he could hear the distant ringing of the telephone, and he counted six times before a voice that was sleepy and remote and familiar answered.

Marion came awake at once when she heard his voice and the words were hurried and urgent as she asked how he was and where he was and what he had been doing.

"Did you find him?" she asked finally.

"He's with me now," he said. "Never mind where. Let's just say we're still in the deep South."

"Will he come?"

"Tomorrow. What about you? Are you all right?"

"No."

"Has the baby—?"

"It's not the baby, it's the police."

He could hear her catch her breath and knew she was fighting her tears. The sound of it made his heart turn over, but before he could speak she said:

"Oh, darling, don't you understand? They're looking for you."

"I know that."

"They think you killed that man. Or I did. They say it was our knife—"

"What?" Hayden heard the word distinctly but in the shock of his surprise he could not accept it. "How can they think that?"

"They say it belongs to that set we have in the kitchen.... They could be right," she added, her voice rough with emotion. "One of ours is missing. I can't find it anywhere."

She said other things along the same line, but he was too stunned to absorb them until she said: "And there's something else, John. That girl at the tavern, Doris Lamar—"

"What about her?"

"She came to see me this evening. She said she knew something that would help us."

"Did you tell the police?"

"She says if I tell the police she'll deny everything. She—she wants money," she added. "She doesn't know who killed Adler but she says she can help us."

"All right." He stopped and made a desperate effort to evaluate what he had heard. He did not understand how this could be nor know just what to say but he wanted to offer some words of comfort and encouragement until he could get home. "What did you tell her?"

"I told her she'd have to wait until you came home."

"Good girl," he said.

"She warned me again not to go to the police—"

"That's all right too. Sit tight, baby. You're wonderful. I'll call you from New York sometime tomorrow afternoon, maybe late. Stick to your story. And call on Roger Denham if you need him."

"But suppose the police find you first."

"They're not going to find me. I'll be back and so will Corbin. We'll work things out. Now please go back to bed and go to sleep. I'm going to do the same."

Some odd reaction born of strain and tension and uncertainty made her giggle softly. "I'm already in bed."

"Then go to sleep."

"I'll try."

"Try hard.... I love you."

CHAPTER 18

THE FLIGHT TO NEW York's Idlewild Airport was a few minutes late taking off from Moisant but lost no more time en route to Washington. Hayden and Corbin, both wearing dark glasses now, did not sit together and exchanged no words until they reclaimed their bags at the terminal. As they stood waiting, Corbin came up to Hayden with a cigarette in his mouth and asked for a light.

"Do we get a car?"

"We do."

"You or me?"

"Have you got a credit card?" Hayden watched the big man nod. "Then you're elected. They won't be looking for you here but they could be looking for me. I'll make a phone call and meet you out front when you're ready."

He moved away, heading along a corridor that would take him to the taxi stand, and stopped at the first public booth he came to. There was no delay in getting the call through and Marion answered almost at once.

"Hi, sweetheart," he said. "Are you alone?"

"Yes, John. Is Ted with you?"

"He's renting a car. Have you been out today?"

"This morning. To do some shopping."

"Do you think you were followed?"

"No."

"No police cars out front or down the road?"

"I don't think so."

"Good," he said, and went on to tell her where to meet them. "We'll be in a sedan with New York plates," he added. "If you're followed, don't stop. Go back home and wait until I can think of something else. If not, take the next right and pull off the road. Got it?"

"Yes, I think so. What time?"

"Five o'clock...."

Luck stayed with them as they crossed the bridge and came sedately up the Hutchinson River Parkway and onto the Merritt. Corbin obeyed all speed laws and they turned north in the fading light of the bleak March day. This was a blacktop road and winding, and when they came finally to the intersection Hayden had specified, he saw the station wagon parked on the shoulder of the road just ahead.

Corbin drew in front of it and stopped. He looked at Hayden. "What does a guy say at a time like this?" he asked.

"You'll think of something. Come on."

They got out and walked back. Hayden opened the door and slid over on the seat and Marion's arms went around his neck to give him a quick, spasmodic hug before she kissed him. She let go reluctantly as Corbin climbed in beside Hayden, her hazel eyes softly curious and a little shy as she inspected the big man who had once been her husband.

"Hello, Marion," he said, and offered his hand. "I thought I could stay lost for good. I thought I was doing you a favor. I'm sorry it didn't work out that way."

She took his hand, held it momentarily, released it.

"I'm sure you did," she said. "You were never cruel or mean or spiteful."

"Just stupid," Corbin said wryly.

"Not that either. I'm awfully glad you came back."

"I owed you that much. But that's not all of it. I have a girl in Alabama," he said, an odd huskiness in his voice. "I was going to marry her. I made a new life as Ted Cannon. I thought it would be all right. It would have been if it hadn't been for—"

He stopped here and they all knew what he meant.

"Maybe you still can," Marion said quietly.

"Yeah."

Hayden believed what he had heard, but there was a growing impatience nagging at his brain and he knew there could not be much more time left. He pressed his wife's arm to get her attention.

"Anything new since last night?"

"I heard from Roger," she said and looked at Corbin. "Did Adler phone you Monday night?"

"Me?" Corbin's blue eyes opened slowly and just as slowly narrowed again. "No."

"Why?" Hayden asked, the old but not forgotten suspicion finding new nourishment. "What did Denham say?"

"The police were checking public telephone booths. They started around here and widened the area. They found the record of a call made to Fairview, Alabama from a booth just outside the Log Cabin Restaurant on the Post Road. I wondered—"

"Not to me," Corbin said.

The denial was no longer good enough for Hayden. Not any more. Monday was the night Adler had taken Doris Lamar out dancing, the night he had slugged George Freeman. Adler had tried to blackmail Corbin in Alabama. He had been thrown out and threatened....

"What about Doris?" he said, new ideas forming in his mind now but wanting to get as much information as he could. "Do you know *how* she can clear us?"

"I don't know if she's telling the truth," Marion said, "but I know what she said. When she came last night she was embarrassed but she was defiant too. It was as if a part of her was ashamed of the way she was acting while another part insisted that she had a right to make the proposition. She said you had already spoken to her about it and she was accepting your offer. She said she knew she was going to be in for some trouble in one way or another, but she might as well get paid for it."

"She must have seen something the night Adler was killed," Hayden said.

"She did. She told them at the tavern that she had a headache and asked for time off to go home and get some special pills she had."

"But she didn't go home," Hayden said, remembering what the woman had told him when he had called at her cottage.

"She started over to see Adler. She thinks it was about twenty-five minutes after eight or maybe eight-thirty. She had just started through that parking space in the center of the motel when she saw Adler's door open. She stopped and stepped behind a car. She saw me come out and hurry past her on my way to get back to where I had parked the station wagon."

"Ahh—" Hayden said.

"What?"

It took him a moment to reply because he had to be careful not only of what he said but how he sounded. His first thought, which was one of overwhelming relief, was mixed with other emotions more difficult to analyze. He had at no time believed that Marion could have killed Adler, but she had lied to him and the business of the knife that she had told him the night before had been burrowing insidiously in the back of his mind ever since. Now, taking a small breath and concentrating on keeping his voice steady, he said:

"I mean, that's wonderful. She went in to see Adler after you'd gone and he was alive. That's perfect. How long was she there?"

"She says it was only a few minutes. Adler started to make a drink. He squeezed a lemon and was looking around for some sugar when they heard this knock at the door. Adler didn't know who it was. He said he wasn't expecting anyone, but Doris thought George Freeman might have seen her and had come there to make trouble. So Adler told her to step into the bathroom and close the door. He said if it was Freeman, he'd get rid of him in a hurry."

She stopped to moisten her lips and her eyes were wide and fixed as they met his own. She seemed not to be trying to build suspense with her hesitation but only searching for words; finally they came.

"That was when it happened," she said. "While she was still in the bathroom."

Again the silence came and this time Hayden broke it. "How long was she there?"

"She's not sure."

"Didn't she hear anything?"

"Just some voices that she couldn't understand or even identify. She didn't hear anyone raise his voice or cry out. She didn't hear the sound of anything falling. All she remembers is that suddenly there weren't any voices any more and she waited another minute or two and finally inched the bathroom door open to take a look. First she thought the room was empty, so she came out and then she saw him."

She continued quickly, relating the things that Doris Lamar had told her and trying to re-create the feeling of shock and horror and fear that had come to the woman.

"When she realized he was dead she got out," she said. "She didn't stop to think whether it was the wise thing to do. She says she was too panicky to think, that she acted on the spur of the moment, and the only thing she had in mind was to get away from there as quick as she could. She came out and shut the door and started for the street and then she saw this man walking past the office and coming her way."

"Yes," Hayden said as he remembered the moment and the impression that had come to him that night. There had been a woman, but he had never seen her or known what had happened to her. "It was me, wasn't it?"

"Yes. She says she hid behind a car and watched you go into the room. The minute the door closed she ran.... Don't you see, darling?" she said, a break in her voice that she could not control. "If Adler was dead before you came—"

He took her arm and squeezed it hard. He said he knew what she meant. Ted Corbin, who had been silent and still during the past minutes, shifted his weight on the seat and cleared his throat.

"You mean this dame knew about this all the time and wouldn't tell the police? What the hell kind of a dame is that?" he demanded of no one in particular. "She knows neither of you did it and yet she'd let you stand trial for murder—"

"No, Ted," Marion cut in, leaning forward slightly, so she could see him better. "She said if we were actually arrested and indicted she would tell the truth.... Oh, she wasn't proud of what she was doing," she added. "She said she wanted to get out of here and she had to have some money. She said she knew she would be in for a hard time with the police for not having told them the truth before, and now she thought she ought to get something for the trouble the police would give her."

Because he knew a little about Doris Lamar, Hayden could understand the situation and accept the motives which had prompted the girl's odd behavior. She could not make up her mind to settle down with George Freeman. There had been a chance to break out with Sam Adler and somebody had taken care of that too. He felt no resentment toward her for having kept her knowledge to herself; what was important was that her co-operation could be had, and now he straightened, his mind made up.

"Okay," he said, "I'll take it from here."

A glance at his watch told him it was a quarter of six. That meant he would have to go to Jerry's Tavern to find Doris, but he did not think it would be difficult to get her outside long enough to tell her how he felt. He mentioned this aloud as he started to lay his plans, and Marion contradicted him.

"She won't be at the tavern," she said. "She told me last night that she quit yesterday."

"That's all the better," Hayden said. "I can talk to her at her place." He looked at Corbin. "Do they know you at the motel?"

"No."

"I'd like to use the rented car if you don't mind."

"Sure. Why not?"

"Marion can drop you off at the motel and you can register and stay in your room until I get in touch with you. It shouldn't be too long."

———◦———

Once in the rented car, Hayden moved circuitously by back roads until he came to the highway approaching the village from the south. Starting about five miles out of town he made inquiries at three filling stations and each time he drew a blank. This brought him finally to Lee Cramer's place, and as he pulled to a stop beside the gasoline pumps he was reminded again of that night four days earlier.

It was the same kind of day, windy and raw, and dusk was settling fast. Lee Cramer looked just the same as he hustled from the shelter of his cubelike office. The chief difference was that Cramer did not recognize the car, and when he was close enough to see who was driving it he seemed to falter and his gaze was both puzzled and curious. The expression suggested that he might well know the authorities were looking for Hayden, but that did not stop his friendly greeting.

"Evening, Mr. Hayden.... New car?"

"A rented one, Lee," Hayden said. "But I don't need any gas. I'm looking for some information and I thought maybe you could help me."

"I can try."

"I'm trying to check on a man that came into town Tuesday night."

"Tuesday?" Lee nodded. "That would be the night the fellow was murdered down at the motel."

"That's right. And this man would be a stranger. He might have stopped to ask the same questions Adler did the night before. I checked at three stations down the road but no one remembers him and I thought you might. A big man, tall, well built, good-looking, with a tan and maybe a touch of southern accent."

Cramer frowned as he considered the question. He looked up at the sky and then at Hayden. He shook his head.

"I can't place him, Mr. Hayden. He didn't stop here, at least not while I was on."

"When do you go off?"

"Around six-thirty usually. My son-in-law—he works in Bridge-port—takes over for me most evenings."

Hayden had to swallow his disappointment but, so long as there was a chance, he could not quit. "Could you call him, Lee? Would he be home now?"

"He should be," Cramer said. "I'll find out."

He hurried off to disappear in the office and Hayden slumped down in the seat and tried to be patient. He needed further corroboration for the idea that had been forming in the back of his mind for the past twenty-four hours, and the expression on Lee Cramer's blocky face when he hurried out of the office gave him new hope.

"That was a good hunch, Mr. Hayden."

"He remembers him?"

"Just like you described him. He pulled in and asked if this was the way to The Shady Maple. He also asked if Frank knew you. Frank said not very well but he knew who you were."

"Does he remember what time it was?"

"He says he thinks it was around eight-thirty but he can't be real sure."

Hayden thanked him. He said he would explain later why the information was important. Then he was accelerating back onto the highway, his confidence mounting as the new and essential part of the mental pattern fell into place. He drove swiftly but with care, and in his mind was the comforting thought that all he needed was a little more time. Give him that and he would be ready for the police and their questions, and it was this thought that took him past the tavern and the motel and brought him to the driveway on the left side of the quiet street.

The archaic and empty mansion had a long-abandoned look now, and it was too dark to read the For Sale sign as he drove past and came to the cottage at the rear. He parked under the trees and switched off his lights, hurrying now, aware that the shades were drawn but seeing a dim crack of illumination in the front.

He was on the step then, knocking, his impatience dominating him. He reached for the knob and when the door opened he pushed into the room. What happened then came without warning.

It was not that instinct failed him; he never gave it a chance. The urgency that had carried him this far had its own momentum, and he was forever grateful that there had been no delay or indecision on his part. For these minutes he had saved proved to be priceless, and in the end his occupation with his thoughts saved him.

There may have been a moment when he was intuitively aware that danger lurked beside him. He also realized too late that he had stepped into darkness and he knew that this should not be. There should have been no darkness, and he now found it both frightening and impenetrable. In that same brief instant he could have heard some movement close by, some whisper of sound that told him something was horribly wrong. Later he knew it must have been that way because he ducked automatically as he tried to check himself and turn toward the unseen threat.

Even as he made his move he was hit and this time the darkness was an ally. The blow missed his head but crashed solidly into the angle of his neck and shoulder, a shocking, vicious smash that knocked him off balance. The topcoat helped cushion the force of the impact, but his effort to turn was much too late and he went down heavily, not hurt but bewildered by the darkness and the unfamiliar surroundings.

He rolled instinctively as he hit the floor. He came to his knees, still not seeing anything. He swore aloud and tried to lunge toward the open door as he came to his feet, but he was moving blindly and fell again as an overturned chair tripped him.

He knew as he finally regained his balance that whoever had attacked him had gone. The night air was in his face as he felt his way to the door and he closed it, hearing nothing outside, knowing that the man had left the way he had come—by foot from the street beyond the wooded area at the rear.

Only then was he really conscious of the quiet surrounding him. Only then was he able to think of Doris Lamar, and he was suddenly so scared and empty inside that he called out to her. He called again, his voice rising, then fumbled frantically along the wall until he found the electric switch.

He blinked against the sudden brightness, and then he saw her, and now the fear was real and paralyzing. She lay crumpled near the center of the room, skirts high and twisted, her face turned away. But even then, unable yet to think or even to move, he could see the stocking knotted about her neck and the dark stain that discolored the bright yellow hair.

CHAPTER 19

THE FEAR THAT HELD John Hayden rooted to the floor in those next awful moments was two-edged and stunning in its impact. For it was not just the sight of the girl and the instant understanding of what must have happened here; it was the realization that without her there would be no testimony to be bought and paid for, no chance for the truth that would clear Marion and himself to be told.

He was moving as the thought hit him, shucking off his coat and tossing it aside, then dropping to one knee and lifting the limp torso while he supported the back of her head. He could feel the warmth of her body against him and he could see now that the stocking held no knot but had simply been twisted across her throat, apparently from the back. He saw the blood above and in back of the temple even though the thickness of the blond hair obscured the wound itself. But it was the color of her face that shocked him most.

There was a grayness beneath the make-up, and he spoke her name again, not knowing that he did so. He touched her cheek and there was warmth there, and he found a wrist and thought he sensed a pulse beat. But she did not seem to be breathing, and he lowered her and turned her face-down, frantic now and driven by a desperation that had as its focus the determination to make her breathe again.

Without experience, not daring to take the time to call a doctor, he moved astride her hips and put both hands beside the rib cage, low down, his fingers pressing and relaxing as he shifted his weight. He found a rhythm of sorts and hoped it was right. He counted, aware of nothing but the warmth of her and the movement he induced.

He was not sure how long it was before he felt a stirring beneath his fingertips. He was not even sure there was a movement at first. He made himself keep to the rhythm but more gently now. Then he felt the response and leaned close, his head beside hers, and heard the faint and labored and wonderful sound of her breathing.

His hands were sweaty and trembling as he caught a breath of his own, and it was then that he felt the cold draft sliding along the floor to touch his spine and make him wonder. Before he could understand this he heard the hoarse cry behind him and the sound of it made his scalp crawl. Somehow he managed to jerk his head around and for a long and terrifying second death stared back at him.

He saw the gun first and it was pointed right at him. He had no time to think, but his reaction was spontaneous and instinctive and he gave voice to it at once. He yelled, the words harsh and violent:

"*George!* Wait! I found her like this. I just got here."

He swallowed in an effort to speak again. He moved aside with great caution, an inch at a time, his gaze fixed on George Freeman's white and twisted face. The back of his neck was cold and there was a great emptiness inside him as he saw the tension in the hand that held the gun and the wild unseeing eyes. He knew he had to get through to the man, to make him see, and now he spoke again, his tone rough, profane, and jarring.

"She's alive," he said. "Help me, goddammit! Put that gun down and give me a hand!"

The face that had always seemed so bland and boyish remained pale and twisted but something happened to the eyes. Something had registered in the mind and there was a flicker of movement, a faint gleam of recognition, as Hayden pressed his advantage.

"Call the police!" he snapped. "Get a doctor and an ambulance. Hurry, damn it!"

That time the words got through. The gun wavered slightly, its muzzle dipping, and he began to breathe again. He could feel the perspiration break out on his forehead, the trickle of it down his sides. He could hear the rapid pulsing of his heart as Freeman finally moved.

"Who did it?" he demanded hoarsely.

"I don't know."

"I'll kill him."

"All right. But call a doctor first."

He turned back to the girl to make sure she was still breathing. There was no sign of consciousness and his helplessness dismayed him. He wanted to do something about the wound on the head, but when he saw there seemed to be no more bleeding he let it alone and listened to Freeman give orders over the phone.

* * *

The first person to arrive in response to George Freeman's telephone call was a uniformed State Policeman, a stone-faced, competent-looking fellow who, after his first quick glance about the room, went directly to the girl. When he straightened he asked a minimum of questions as he stepped over to the telephone. He was still talking when the doctor arrived.

Hayden, who had sat down on the couch because of the odd weakness in the back of his legs, watched the man take off his hat and coat and then move over to kneel beside the girl. He spent some time parting the blond hair and examining the wound; finally he pointed to the mark on her throat. He picked up the stocking that Hayden had discarded and glanced around.

"Did somebody try to strangle her?"

Hayden said he thought so. He explained where he had found the stocking and what he had done.

"I thought she was alive," he said, "but I couldn't tell whether she was breathing or not, so I tried to give her artificial respiration."

"It did no harm," the doctor said, "and it might have helped." He cocked his head and Hayden heard the distant wail of a siren. It faded as he listened, but now there was a sound of a car moving down the driveway and the doctor said: "If that's the ambulance will you ask them to come right in?"

Freeman, who had been standing near the door and saying nothing, turned and went out. When he returned he was followed by two men with a stretcher and blankets. As they put the stretcher down beside the girl the State Policeman spoke.

"Maybe the lieutenant ought to see her, Doc," he said.

"I think it's more important that we get her into oxygen right away," the doctor replied and gave a silent signal to the two men.

They lifted her gently onto the stretcher and tucked a blanket about her. At a nod from the doctor they raised the stretcher, and as they started out he said he would call the hospital and alert them.

He had just finished with the telephone when Lieutenant Garvey came in with another officer who was also in plainclothes, a blocky, black-browed man a few years younger than his superior. He saw Hayden in his first all-inclusive glance, but if he felt any surprise it did not show. He apparently had been given some information either by telephone or radio and he now turned directly to the doctor.

"How bad is she?"

"Hard to tell." The doctor glanced at Hayden. "I believe he can give you the details. All I can tell is that she has a concussion, possibly a severe one. We can't know about a fracture until we've taken some pictures."

"Will she live?"

"I'd say she has a reasonable chance." He gestured with one hand. "But concussions are tricky. It's not a sure thing by any means."

"How long before she'll be conscious?"

"Maybe an hour. Maybe a day, a week, maybe never."

When the door closed behind the doctor, Garvey gave his full attention to Hayden. He took his time, the deep-set gray eyes probing and intent, his lips compressed but not grim.

"Have a good trip?" he asked dryly.

"I think it was worthwhile."

"What makes you think so?"

"I got what I went after," Hayden said. "I brought Corbin back with me."

"Corbin?" Garvey considered the name. "That would be Mrs. Hayden's first husband? Where did you locate him?"

"In Fairview, Alabama."

"That's across the Bay from Mobile. You must have beat the local boys to it."

"But not by much."

"Did you fly out of Mobile?"

"New Orleans."

"That was smart. You knew they were looking for him."

"I knew they were looking for me."

"How long have you been back?"

"About an hour."

Garvey nodded and his attitude was suddenly more businesslike than skeptical. "Okay, we'll get to that later. What brought you here? What happened?"

Hayden told him, and it was an easy thing to do because the scene was still so vivid in his mind. Garvey listened without interruption, his gray gaze speculative but attentive until the story was over.

"You thought you saw a light in here when you got out of the car," he said, "but when you walked in it was dark."

"That's right. Before I had a chance to wonder about it he jumped me."

"Then if you'd been a couple of minutes later he would have finished the job on the girl." He thought it over a minute, his lips pursing. "You were trying to give her artificial respiration when George Freeman walked in on you, is that right?"

"I'd just finished."

"And he had a gun?" He glanced about the room and suddenly his eyes narrowed and he looked at the plainclothes man who had come with him. "Where is he, Malone?"

"The last I saw of him he went in there." Malone pointed to the bedroom. "I thought he was going to the john."

"Take a look," Garvey said and waited until the detective returned alone, a sheepish expression on his face. "Take a look outside." He watched the other leave and turned back to Hayden. "What brought you here in the first place?"

"Is it important?"

"It could be."

Hayden stood up and reached for a cigarette, his brown eyes somber and troubled as he considered his reply. Then, because it was something that had to be done, he decided to tell the truth.

"If Doris Lamar doesn't live I can't prove this," he said, "but Doris came to my wife and told her she had information that would clear both of us. She said she would deny it if my wife went to you. She wanted money and she said she was willing to take her chances on any trouble you could give her if she got paid for what she knew. I came here to find out how much she wanted."

The skepticism still showed on Garvey's face. He asked other questions and Hayden answered them. He was still at it when Malone came back and shook his head and now Garvey said: "All right, we'll pick him up later."

Before he could continue Hayden spoke. "I'd like to ask a favor."

"Such as what?"

"There's a lot of talking to be done," he said, "so why couldn't we do it at my place instead of here?"

"Why?"

"I told you I brought Corbin back with me. He should be at The Shady Maple now. You're going to want to question him because he knows a lot about Sam Adler. My wife still doesn't know how Corbin happened to miss that plane in Capitol City two years ago. She doesn't know what Corbin did and what was happening during those years.

"Also," he continued, "I've got some ideas about Corbin myself. I understand that my wife and I are still under some suspicion of murder and I'd like to get out from under. So why not go down to my place and have it out in one session? If you don't mind, I'd like to get my lawyer there too, just in case."

Such arguments had a reasonable sound and even Garvey seemed impressed. He glanced at Malone, then back at Hayden. For another second or two he hesitated as the logic behind the request came through to him and a glimmer of something that might have been respect replaced the doubt in his gray eyes.

"Call your lawyer," he said. "You may need him. Tell him to meet you at your place."

He belted his trench coat as Hayden dialed Roger Denham's number and stated his request. When he hung up, Garvey was waiting.

"Get your coat," he said. "I'll pick up Corbin. Would he be registered under that name?"

"He's been using the name Cannon for the past couple of years," Hayden said. "You could try that first, but whoever's on the desk should remember him."

Garvey nodded again. "I'll get him, and Freeman if I can find him. Malone can ride with you," he added. "Like you said—just in case.... Okay?"

CHAPTER 20

JOHN HAYDEN HAD HOPED that he would be able to talk to Marion alone before Lieutenant Garvey took charge of the investigation, but there was nothing he could do about it now. He could see the uncertainty in the hazel eyes when she saw Malone, and he had no choice but to introduce the detective and tell her that Garvey was on his way over with Ted Corbin.

By the time he had taken care of their coats and Malone had settled himself on the divan, the doorbell rang and he went over to admit Roger Denham. The lawyer's bespectacled gaze was bright and curious, but he shook hands warmly when he stepped inside.

"I'm certainly glad to see you," he said. "When I got your note and found out what you intended to do I thought it was a foolish move, but Marion tells me you pulled it off. Where's Corbin now?"

"At the motel. Lieutenant Garvey's bringing him over—that is, if he hasn't skipped."

He introduced Malone and took Denham's coat, and then he spoke of Doris Lamar. He kept his account of what had happened as brief as he could, seeing the surprise in Denham's eyes and the look of shock and incredulity in his wife's face. To give her some encouragement, he stopped beside her chair to take her hand.

"She's still alive," he said. "She has a chance."

"But if—"

"Don't think that way," he cut in. "I've told the lieutenant what she told you and—"

"But I don't understand. Who could have done it, John? Who?"

He had no chance to answer the question, and for this he was grateful because he was not ready for it. He came quickly to his feet as the doorbell rang again, and then Lieutenant Garvey and Ted Corbin were in the room and it was time for Garvey to take the floor.

Once again he declined Hayden's offer to take his coat, but he opened it and sat down, putting his hat beside the chair.

"Detective Ball is at the hospital with the Lamar woman," he said. "We may hear something, we may not. I understand one of you"—he glanced at Corbin and then back at Hayden—"is going to tell me why Corbin disappeared. You're going to tell me what Adler knew about that disappearance. But first I'd like to ask *you* some questions, Mr. Hayden."

He paused, the gray eyes steady, and something in that look told Hayden he wasn't going to like the questions.

"You went to Mobile and Fairview to look for Corbin. That means you knew he was alive."

"I thought he might be."

"What made you think so?"

It was Hayden's turn to hesitate, and when he understood that evasion and temporizing would get him nowhere he decided to do the best he could with the truth.

"Adler came to my wife and told her so."

"He wanted money to stay quiet about it?"

"Yes."

"She told you. You went to Mr. Denham for advice and then you went to The Shady Maple. Now what took you to Mobile? How did you know Adler might have come from there?"

"You told me later."

Garvey's brows lifted. "So I did. All right. Now assuming Corbin lived in that area, how did you expect to find him? No one knew him by that name. You had to have some kind of a lead, a photograph or something—"

Hayden was already reaching for the snapshots and the enlargement of the insignia on the coveralls Corbin had worn when the picture was taken. He offered them, saw Garvey's eyes narrow as he inspected them.

"You took them from Adler's wallet," the lieutenant said. "You denied being there that night."

"I had to deny it. If you had known what Adler wanted then, and there was always a chance those negatives would turn up—as a matter of fact they did—then you would have known I had both a motive for murder and the opportunity. You might have arrested me that first night."

"We might have.... So how did you finally locate Corbin?"

Hayden told him in detail about his search the previous day, and when he finished Garvey cleared his throat.

"Now that we've got that part straight let's let it go for now and get back to Adler and how *he* knew Corbin was alive."

Hayden looked over at Corbin, who was sitting in his chair, supported by shoulders and buttocks, his long legs stretched out with ankles crossed.

"Do you want to tell it?"

Corbin lifted one hand, tipped it. A small smile twisted his tanned, good-looking face and his voice was unconcerned.

"Go ahead. You're better with words than I am."

Hayden reached for a straight-backed chair and sat down. He said what he had to say was going to take quite a while and to make any sense he would have to explain why Corbin had decided to disappear when the opportunity came to him.

He spoke as briefly as he could about the marriage that could no longer survive and the circumstances which had taken Corbin to Capitol City in the first place. Recalling all the things that the big man had told him, he re-created a verbal picture that included the money Corbin had won with his football bets, the trench coat, the offering of that coat to the man who had none, the timing of Corbin's movements in the air terminal that made it possible for the stranger to board the plane in his place.

He did the best he could with Corbin's thoughts and movements, once he heard the aircraft had crashed. He spoke of the bus trip from the airport to Capitol City and from there to Mobile. He told of Adler's curiosity, his feeling that if he was patient and played his cards right he might someday be rewarded for what he knew.

"The newspaper accounts told him about Marion and the insurance money," he said. "For two years he continued to check on her and Corbin. He knew she had married again; he knew about me. He also knew that Corbin had done pretty well and that he had a girl he expected to marry. He took a snapshot and got a photograph of Corbin's fingerprints and then he was ready for the payoff."

He stopped, aware that he had been talking a long time, that the back of his throat was dry. He glanced over at Roger Denham in his well-tailored, three-button suit. Corbin was still stretched out in his chair and Marion, sitting in the opposite corner of the divan from Garvey, had pulled her legs up under her, her knees bent. Neither Garvey nor Malone had interrupted him, and now he concentrated on arranging the facts as he knew them so he could bring the story up to date.

"Adler went to Corbin first," he said. "He told him what he knew and promised to stay quiet for five thousand dollars. He had a gun with him but Corbin took it away and threw him out and threw the gun after him. He warned him if he opened his mouth again he would wind up in Mobile Bay with an anchor around his neck. I think Adler believed him. I think he'd had enough of Corbin, so he came North to see how much he could collect from us."

He took a breath and said: "But Adler wouldn't let well enough alone. He resented the treatment Corbin had given him and he was now fifteen hundred miles away. Being the kind of person he was, he couldn't resist telephoning Corbin and telling him that he was going to collect anyway.... You found out about that phone call, didn't you?" he said to Garvey.

Garvey considered the question and decided to answer it affirmatively.

"It came from a booth near the Log Cabin," Hayden said. "It was made on the night Adler took Doris Lamar there, the night George Freeman tried to jump him. I think that call was to Corbin and it was a mistake because Corbin flew up here to stop him."

"Now wait a minute." Corbin pulled in his legs, put his hands on the chair arms, and lifted himself to a sitting position. He leaned forward slightly, brows bent and his jaw hard. "Just because Adler called me doesn't mean I came."

Hayden stood up and produced the baggage tag he had removed from the big man's suitcase the night before when Corbin had gone to see his girl for a few minutes. He gave the tag to Garvey.

"Corbin had to stop Adler," he said. "What was happening was his fault and he wasn't just thinking about himself. He didn't want Marion to get hurt for something he did if he could help it."

Garvey inspected the tag, turned it over, and he needed no diagram. He looked at Corbin.

"This says you flew from New York to Mobile Wednesday morning. That means you were probably in New York Tuesday night."

"I can take it a little farther than that," Hayden said. "I can *prove* he was in town Tuesday night." He paused, conscious of Corbin's stare, but when there was no interruption he explained how he had checked the filling stations that afternoon and what he had learned from Lee Cramer.

"Cramer's son-in-law remembers Corbin," he said. "He can identify him if necessary. So I say Adler not only made the mistake of bragging about what he was going to do, he also told Corbin where he was staying. Corbin asked directions to The Shady Maple. He was looking for Adler and—"

"So what?" Corbin cut in harshly, his tanned face shiny with perspiration. "That doesn't mean I killed him."

"When he told me how he had threatened Adler in Fairview," Hayden said to Garvey, "an expression he used bothered me. I suppose it's only a matter of semantics and it certainly isn't proof, but I remember the sentence. He said: '*I should have killed him then.*'" He paused to make sure they understood him. "Why should he say it that way? Why should he use the word *then*? Why not simply: 'I should have killed him'?"

Garvey coughed and the sound of it got their attention. "You admit being here that night, Mr. Corbin?"

"I guess I have to," Corbin said. "But that's all I'll admit. Sure I stopped at the filling station and asked where The Shady Maple was. But I didn't register. I never stepped on the property. I guess it was around a quarter of nine when I parked and I was hungry. I wanted some time to think, so I went over to the tavern and had a couple of drinks and a sandwich. By the time I had finished the police cars were in the street. There were a few people out there watching and I asked somebody what had happened and they told me."

He swallowed visibly and said, a note of desperation in his voice: "I hung around just long enough to find out who had been killed. I knew how it would look if I got caught there, so I got the hell out. I drove back to the airport and spent the night in a motel and took the nine-thirty plane out in the morning."

Garvey looked at Hayden. "Did you actually talk with Lee Cramer's son-in-law?"

"I talked with Lee," Hayden said. "I waited while he telephoned the son-in-law and that's what he said."

Garvey stood up and began to belt his trench coat. He nodded at Malone and the plainclothes man was already reaching for his coat. He looked at Corbin, who had leaned forward in his chair, a shocked, incredulous look stamped on his face.

"You'd better come along with us, Mr. Corbin."

"But I'm telling you the truth," Corbin said.

"You'll have a chance to prove it."

For another second or two the big man remained where he was. He looked at Hayden and at Marion and then, as though it occurred to him that no one here could help him, he stood up, his jaw set.

"All right," he said, "but I want a lawyer." He looked at Denham. "How about you?"

Denham came to his feet. "This sort of thing is a little out of my line," he said, "but I can recommend someone." He took a notebook from his pocket and wrote a few lines with an automatic pencil. He passed the slip of paper to Corbin. "Both of these are good men," he said. "If you have trouble reaching them, call me."

Corbin pocketed the piece of paper and went over to get his coat. He put it on and made a final effort to convince Garvey.

"I admit Adler called me," he said. "I came up here."

"To stop him."

"Well—yes. I suppose so."

"You didn't care how?"

"I didn't think about that. I only knew I couldn't let him foul up Marion's life for something that was my fault. I didn't stop to think how I was going to stop him, but I scared the hell out of him once and I figured to do it again."

"All right, Mr. Corbin," Garvey said quietly, "you'll have your chance to prove that."

The telephone rang in time to punctuate the sentence, and there was a moment of silence as they all exchanged glances at the unexpected sound. When Hayden stepped over to answer it a man's voice asked for Lieutenant Garvey, and he turned to offer the telephone. They stood listening self-consciously as Garvey said:

"Yeah.... Wait a minute." He put the telephone down beside the cradle and looked at Hayden. "Would there be an extension?"

"In the bedroom," Hayden said, and led the way.

When he came back he saw that Marion had come to her feet and was standing close to Ted Corbin, not touching him but looking up at him, her smooth brow furrowed now with concern and the hazel eyes compassionate. They seemed not to be aware of anyone else in the room at the moment and he heard her say:

"I'm so sorry, Ted."

"Forget it," Corbin said, his voice gruff. "It's my own damn fault."

"But—you came up here to help me."

"Why not? Just because we couldn't cut it as man and wife doesn't mean I don't still like you. I've always liked you; you know that. And, what the hell, I'm the guy that had that brilliant idea two years ago."

"I'm not blaming you for that."

"I know you're not." He reached out and took her hand. "And whatever happens, don't worry about the divorce thing. We can work something out in a hurry and—"

He stopped as the door opened and Lieutenant Garvey came back into the room. He let go of Marion's hand and stepped aside. And Hayden, seeing the lieutenant's frown, felt an odd tingle of excitement that had come from nowhere and was motivated by nothing more than the expression on Garvey's face.

"That was Detective Ball from the hospital," he said, taking time to look at Hayden and then at Marion. "The Lamar girl was conscious for a little while and Ball had a stenographer with him."

"Is she going to be all right?" Marion asked quickly.

"They're not sure about that part," Garvey said, "but she did tell Ball a few things.... You're a couple of lucky people," he said and the frown went away. "She corroborated the story she told you. She says Adler was alive when you left, Mrs. Hayden, and she insists that he was dead"—he glanced at Hayden—"when she saw you step into that motel room."

"Does—she know who tried to kill her?" Hayden asked.

"She says no." Garvey looked at Corbin. "Ready, Mr. Corbin?... You don't need to come to the door," he added to Hayden. "We know the way out."

CHAPTER 21

FOR SEVERAL SECONDS AFTER the outer door closed there was nothing but silence in the room. Each seemed busy with his own thoughts and their glances were averted. In his own mind, Hayden was aware of his tangled ideas and an odd sense of frustration mingled with the relief that had come when he knew Doris Lamar had told her story. He also knew what he wanted to do but he was not sure how to go about it, and when the air of depression that hung in the room finally made itself felt he broke it abruptly and with determination.

"I need a drink," he said, and looked at his wife.

She nodded, took a breath with lips tight, and expelled it forcibly. "Me too, please.... Roger?"

Denham went back to his chair, his smile diffident as he considered the invitation. "You know how it is with me but—well, all right. A weak Scotch and soda."

Hayden wheeled and headed for the kitchen. It seemed strangely cool as he entered, but he did not wonder about it until he was back at the sink working on an ice tray. When he finally became conscious of the change, he turned slowly and noticed that the door to the breezeway was ajar. He closed it automatically without thinking any more about it, and went on to pour the drinks. He had them made before his glance touched the knife rack and stopped to focus there as he saw the one empty space.

Denham thanked him for the drink, and Hayden went over and sat down beside his wife. He wanted to say "Cheers" but found the word distasteful, so he merely lifted his glass, nodded, and drank as Marion responded. She lowered her glass and sighed again, the hazel eyes still despairing.

"I simply can't believe it," she said. "Maybe it's because I don't want to believe it."

"If you mean Corbin," Denham said, "he looks to me as if he could be a pretty rough character with the proper provocation."

"I suppose he could be. But that poor girl—"

"Did he know she had offered to give you an alibi for a price?"

"Why"—she glanced at Hayden—"yes, I guess he did." She spoke of their conversation in the station wagon when they had parked on the back road. "I told John and Ted the same thing I told you."

"I suppose he felt he couldn't take a chance," Denham said. "She admitted being in the motel bathroom when Adler was murdered. Maybe Corbin thought she might have known something else that would incriminate him. If he had that in mind it would be easy enough to ask someone where she lived. It's only a couple of blocks from the motel."

Marion shook her head and remained unconvinced. She had her chin up and her mouth had a stubborn twist that Hayden had seen before when she was upset about something.

"I'll never believe it," she said. "With that man Adler it could have happened. He might have threatened Ted or pushed him too far. But not that girl. I lived with him three years. I should know what he was like. He wouldn't hurt a woman, not deliberately. No." She gave her dark hair another toss. "I don't believe it."

Hayden took a small breath and knew it was time for him to give her some help. "Neither do I," he said.

"Oh, come now." Denham's smile was superior, his tone condescending. "It's not what you want to believe that matters. All facts point to Corbin and you both know it. If he didn't, who did?"

"I think you did, Roger," Hayden said. "I think it had to be you."

He heard Marion's small gasp, saw the grin fix itself on Denham's face. Behind the glasses the pale eyes had strange lights in them as they narrowed coldly.

"That's not very funny."

"I agree," Marion added. "What on earth are you talking about?"

"I'm saying Roger killed Adler."

Again he heard the quick words of protest, and when he made no comment a sort of delayed reaction set in and he felt the tension start to build in the room as they realized he meant what he said. He could feel his wife's eyes upon him, but he was watching Denham and he heard him laugh derisively.

"You're out of your mind," he said finally. "Why should I do that?"

"Because you're sick," Hayden said. "You must have been sick for a long time."

"Sick?" Denham said. "You're babbling. I was healthy enough to lead a Ranger outfit in Korea and I've kept myself fit ever since. I'm in better shape right now than you ever were."

"The sickness I'm talking about is in your head, Roger. Who was it you hated most? Was it Marion, or me, or both of us?"

"John!" Marion said, her voice sharp. "Look at me." She waited until Hayden obeyed. "You're wrong. Roger couldn't hate us. He was my friend."

"That's what we thought," Hayden said.

"But why should he kill Adler? He never knew the man, never even talked to him."

"That's what made the plan so good. But if he killed Adler, and I say he did, there can only be one motive." He looked at Denham. "Do you want to know what I think?"

"Not particularly." Denham leaned back and crossed his knees. "But if you insist I'll listen."

"You were in love with Marion once," Hayden said, "if anyone as cold-blooded, self-centered, and stiff-necked as you could ever be in love. She must have sensed that because, while she accepted you as a friend and companion, she wanted no part of you physically. You couldn't get to first base and you couldn't understand it. You had a fine background, social position, money, intelligence, and reasonable good looks, and what happened? She married someone from the other side of the tracks who had nothing much to offer except that physical attraction and a certain personal warmth.

"That marriage didn't work out," he added quickly, "and that must have pleased you. After that plane crash you stood by as the family friend and you probably figured that this time you could get what you wanted. Instead of that, she married someone who, according to your standards, didn't have much more to offer than Corbin. So the hate and bitterness kept eating away at you and there was nothing you could do about it, nothing. No way you could pay Marion back until Sam Adler showed up and gave you a chance."

He took a breath, aware of Denham's bright and narrowed stare but no longer bothered by it. "It wasn't enough that he could prove Corbin was alive and complicate our marriage until something could be worked out. It wasn't enough that I would have to go into debt for a long time to repay the seventy-five thousand dollars Marion had collected. You saw a chance to make one or both of us stand trial for murder. You were going to hang something on us that we'd never live down, and you might have made it if it hadn't been for Doris Lamar. Sam Adler meant nothing to you. You'd killed men before in Korea. Adler was only a means to an end, and you killed him the same way you set up the frame for us—cruelly, deliberately, without compunction, without pity."

"John!"

Again Marion interrupted him and he saw that her face was pale, the eyes stricken by what she had heard.

"You're guessing," she said. "You're making it up."

"All right," Hayden said, "I'm guessing. But I'm not making up the fact that Adler was killed with a knife from our kitchen. Is that right? That's what the police say, isn't it?"

"Yes, but—"

"So who but Roger could have taken that knife? Not Corbin. He didn't get into town until that evening. Not George Freeman."

He could tell by the look on her face that he had scored this time and he continued, ignoring Denham.

"Only you and I and Roger knew why Sam Adler was here and what he wanted. Roger was your good friend," he added, unable to keep the bitterness and resentment from his tone. "You told him everything. He knew where Adler was staying. He knew about the photographs Adler had. He knew I was coming to see him and he felt sure I would go to the motel to have it out with Adler after I'd left him. When I came home Tuesday night and went out to the kitchen to make a drink that knife was missing. I didn't think much about it then. I didn't even consider it until you told me the police thought it came from our kitchen.

"You had already had a drink when I came in Tuesday," he added. "Roger had been here and knew the story. You'd had a drink with him, and he must have been in the kitchen with you. That's when he took the knife. That's the only time he could have taken it, so he must have known then that he was going to kill Adler and frame us if he got the chance. I don't know what his original plan was, but I made it easier for him."

He looked at Denham. "Didn't I, Roger? When I left you Tuesday night I told you I was going to stop at the tavern and get a double brandy before I went over to have it out with Adler. I wanted a little time to pull myself together and that was all you needed. You must have followed a minute or so later. You knew exactly where to find Adler. What you had to do couldn't have taken more than another minute or two. You thought the police would find the snapshots on him and discover what they meant. You knew they'd eventually trace the knife. You were on your way home before I even left the tavern. Luck was with you all the way except for one thing—Doris Lamar."

He paused again, the tension winding a little tighter inside him and the bitterness he could no longer control edging his words.

"Marion still counted on your help and she told you the proposition Doris made. She said so a few minutes ago when you asked if Corbin knew about Doris. You were going to kill her too, not because she could put the finger on you, but because you knew that if she talked she would give us both alibis and that might make the police consider you. With her dead we would be in exactly the same position you set up for us. One or both of us would probably eventually have stood trial for murder and that was what you wanted. That was what you had to have. Two minutes longer and you would have made it, but you didn't dare go after her until it was dark and I got there before you could finish the job."

Denham uncrossed his legs and sat up. If he was concerned by what he heard it did not show. His control and reactions were superb, and except for a tightness around the mouth and the bright, pitiless glints in his eyes there seemed to be no outward change in his appearance.

"What was all the business with Ted Corbin for?" The words were measured and sardonic. "What was the idea of trying to make a case against him with the police?"

"What I said about him was true," Hayden replied. "But when the police check him out at the tavern they will probably find out he is in the clear and that will bring them back to the knife again, Roger. I've read about people who brooded over some injustice, real or fancied, and built up a personal private hate until it became a phobia or a fixation or a neurosis. I wanted to find out how it was with you. I wanted Marion to know the truth about you once and for all."

The remarks did not seem to bother Denham. He ran his fingers through his short, brown hair, and from what he said then it was apparent that he had not heard much of what Hayden had just said.

"You said I had a bad break with Doris Lamar," he said. "I made one other mistake and that was about you, John."

"Yeah," said Hayden. "I've got the picture. I live a well-ordered life. I have no real drive, no spark; I'm dull, conventional, law-abiding. A peasant."

Again Denham did not seem to hear him. There was, somehow, a far-out look in the cold, bespectacled eyes. They were directed at Hayden, but he was not sure they actually saw him, and the look was suddenly disturbing.

"I misjudged you," Denham said in the same, toneless voice. "I fixed the door latch so you could walk in on Adler. I thought when you did and found out what happened you'd be too shocked—maybe stupid is the word—to do anything but call the police. That's what the average levelheaded citizen would do. Why not you?"

"I wasn't very levelheaded at the time," Hayden said. "I was thinking of Marion, and myself, and Ted Corbin. I looked for the snapshots and I found them. I might have destroyed them and called the police then. That's what I wanted to do—until I remembered that if there were snapshots there had to be negatives. When I couldn't find them in the room—"

"That was smart," Denham said. "And the Mobile police did find the negatives. But that took a little time. That gave you a chance to get down and locate Corbin."

The disturbance which had been caused by Denham's strange behavior had ominous side effects, and with them came a warning Hayden could no longer ignore. It seemed now that the sickness he had mentioned still lingered in Denham's mind, and he suddenly wanted to be rid of the man. He took a swallow of his drink and put the glass down. He stood up.

"I think the police will eventually catch up with you," he said. "But you're a lawyer; maybe you can talk your way out of it. Maybe it would be simpler if I called them now and got them over here." He started to turn away, then stopped abruptly as Denham spoke.

"Not just yet, John."

Still sitting erect in the chair and not hurrying, he shifted his weight to one hip. He slid his hand down past the raised hip and found something between the cushion and the chair. When his hand came up it held an automatic pistol. There was a certain familiarity in the way he handled the gun, and now he pointed it at Hayden.

"I took this from Sam Adler," he said, and a small, mean smile twisted one corner of his mouth. "Now I'm rather glad I kept it. Let's talk a little more, John. You sit over here." He gestured with the gun. "I'll sit with Marion and keep an eye on you."

CHAPTER 22

THE SIGHT OF THE gun held John Hayden stiff-legged and immobile for a moment until he realized it had been hidden in the chair some time earlier. Now, accepting the situation, he was surprised to find that he felt no great sense of shock. He glanced at Marion and saw that her face was slack and incredulous. She seemed unable to pull her gaze from Denham, but if there was any feeling of fear inside her it did not yet show. She was, it seemed, not yet ready to accept the fact that this man was indeed sick, and Hayden was glad for that.

"All right," he said, and began to move toward the dining end of the room while Denham circled cautiously toward the divan. "Let's talk. You took the gun from Adler. Is that what you used to slug Doris Lamar?"

Denham nodded as he sat down. "I imagine a laboratory test or a spectrographic analysis may prove it. That's why I brought it when you phoned."

"You intended to plant it?"

"It seemed like a good idea. If Doris failed to recover—and I thought she might—the authorities would have to keep the pressure on you. I felt sure they'd make another search here. If they found the gun it might help clinch the case."

Hayden eased down on the edge of the chair, the back of his neck tightening. For he understood beyond all doubt that Denham's mental instability was no longer academic, and in the brief silence that followed while he tried to collect his thoughts he turned his head slightly, wondering if he had heard some faint sound from the kitchen or whether it was his imagination.

Denham, seeing the movement, mistook its purpose. "Don't try anything, John," he warned. "I've gone too far to make any more mistakes."

"Roger!" Marion found her voice but a look of awe tempered the alarm that now showed in the hazel eyes. "Why, Roger? Why should you hate me so? What did I ever do—?"

"You laughed at me," Denham said, and for the first time there were signs of strain and vindictiveness in his voice as his thoughts focused on the seeds of his sickness. "I tried to be nice, to make love to you, to make you treat me like a man wants to be treated, and you laughed."

"No, Roger."

"I say you did. I had things to offer that most girls want," he added, his words low and ragged now. "But you took Corbin, and Hayden. You wouldn't let me touch you—"

"I didn't laugh, Roger. I didn't want to hurt your feelings. When we were young I liked and admired you. I trusted you. Later I had to be more careful because I knew how you felt. I tried to make you understand that I didn't feel the same way about you. I couldn't help how I felt but I tried to disguise it because we were friends. I tried to explain that the physical thing between a man and a woman is something that is either there or it isn't. It isn't enough for a man to be handsome or considerate or generous. There has to be something very special, and if it's not there you can't pretend that it is; at least I couldn't."

"You laughed."

"No. I liked you too much to tell you that I couldn't stand to have you kiss me. I tried to play it lightly and hoped you'd finally understand. Maybe I shouldn't have. I thought if you'd only accept the fact that I could never be serious about you that way, you'd start looking for someone who could give you what you wanted willingly. Maybe I should have come right out a long time ago and told you. Maybe I should have told you that I could never love you physically, that something about you repelled rather than attracted me, but I didn't want to hurt you—and—"

"That's it," Denham cut in. "You couldn't stand me. You cringed when I touched you, as if there was something rotten inside me. That's what you thought, isn't it?"

"I never stopped to think what it was, Roger. I know now that it must have been something hard and arrogant that made me uneasy and sometimes a little frightened." She caught her breath. "But why did you pretend to be my friend all these years when you hated me?"

"I told you," Hayden said. "He's sick. He's always had exactly what he wanted except you. He couldn't take it. His ego hurt him. He had to get even."

"I waited a long time," Denham said, his voice low but sinister now. "I thought you'd learned your lesson when you and Corbin made such a mess of things. I thought the accident would wake you up and give me another chance. I was even ready to be second choice. I took care of all the details for you. I collected your insurance and nothing had changed. You still pulled away from me when I tried to be affectionate. To make it worse you married Hayden. You turned that money over to him—"

Hayden interrupted. He did not know what Denham's plans were, or if he had any, but he wanted to get the pressure off Marion. He knew that the man would not hesitate to use the gun if he made up his mind, but somehow he was no longer afraid of it.

"Sure," he said, "and that must have burned you plenty. It not only gave me a chance to buy into a business but the business is doing fine."

Denham ignored him. It was as if he had not heard what was said. Whatever lay in his mind was a corrosive thing that was undermining his sanity and there was no room left for digressions.

"Adler gave me the chance I was waiting for," he said, still watching Marion. "When you told me what he wanted and why he was here I knew how to get even."

"You took the knife when you were here," Hayden said.

"I planned to get him right *after* you'd seen him, but when you said you'd stop for a drink at the tavern I decided I could do the job then."

"It didn't bother you a bit, did it?"

"Why should it? I killed better men than him in Korea. He was nothing, a human leech. It was all over before he knew what had happened."

"He never had a chance."

"No chance at all," Denham said, and something about the connotation of the words made them sound as if he were enjoying the thought. "We used to have to do it at night. We had to be quiet. We had to be careful or get killed. But the technique was the same."

The grin that warped his mouth showed his teeth, and to Hayden it seemed that the bright gleam in the pale eyes was no longer rational.

"If I had a knife I could show you, John," he said. "I could demonstrate how easy it is to spin a man around and get your left hand over his mouth from behind while you do the job with your right—"

"Oh, Roger—" Marion buried her face in her hands and for a moment Hayden thought she was going to break down. He heard the muffled sob as she caught her breath, and then she dropped her hands and her face came up, white and stricken. But she was looking right at Denham now when she spoke and her voice had an outraged sound. "How could you?"

"It was almost the same with Doris Lamar," Hayden said, and wondered again if he had not heard some faint whisper of sound from the kitchen. "After you slugged her—how come she didn't get a look at you?—you used the stocking from behind, the way they taught you in the Rangers, hunh?"

"If it had got dark a few minutes earlier I'd have made it."

"You couldn't let her talk, could you? If she told the truth, and you knew she probably would, we'd have been in the clear and you'd have done your killing for nothing. The fact that she was a woman who had never done anything to you made no difference at all."

"Why should it?" Denham said. "As a woman she was no better than Adler. She was amoral, promiscuous, common. She was nothing but a tramp and—"

That was as far as Denham got and Hayden knew that he had not been wrong about the faint sounds he had heard in the kitchen. He heard the sudden violent rush of someone coming through the open door, and even before he could turn he knew who it was, who it had to be. For only one person had a deep and personal feeling about what happened to Doris Lamar, and as he twisted and got a glimpse of George Freeman he knew why he was here.

Later, when he had a chance to think, he understood the compulsive and perhaps irrational drive that precipitated the outburst. To Freeman Doris Lamar was none of the things that Denham had just mentioned. Freeman was in love with the girl; he had already proved it when he tangled with Sam Adler at the Log Cabin.

He could not know then whether Doris would live or die, but he had sworn to kill whoever was responsible. To give himself that chance he had sneaked away from her cottage earlier. He had known that they were all coming here and the door to the breezeway, which had been ajar earlier, was evidence of how he had entered. He knew now that Denham was responsible. He had heard the woman he loved maligned and slandered and he was ready for the showdown.

Hayden could not stop him. He saw the gun that Freeman had threatened him with before. The round face was chalky and stiff and the eyes held that same wild, unseeing look. He was yelling now as he snapped up the gun and the words made no sense to Hayden.

There was only time for him to feel the full impact of a paralyzing fear that was directed not at himself but at Marion before the gun kicked in Freeman's hand and the sound of it slammed through the room.

He knew at once that Freeman had missed. He heard the second shot, but by then Denham, who had been under fire before, was moving.

He rolled sideways off the end of the divan and came to a stop in a crouch. The sound of a door opening somewhere in the distance caught Hayden's ear, though he did not understand it, and with it Denham squeezed the trigger.

Hayden saw the gun buck in Denham's hand. He heard Freeman's third shot and knew that Denham had still not been hit. But Freeman had. The bullet struck him somewhere high on the right side, the impact jerking his shoulder back and staggering him slightly.

Denham, still in the crouch, a gleam of some inner satisfaction brightening his bespectacled gaze, seemed about to fire again when Hayden heard the shouts of warning.

Somehow he managed to pull his horrified gaze from Marion, who had instinctively ducked forward to lower her head in her lap. He saw Lieutenant Garvey and the plainclothes man named Malone at the end of the room. He saw their service revolvers snap up and swing toward Denham. He heard two voices, the two quick, hard commands spoken simultaneously.

"Hold it!... Drop it!"

There was no hesitation on Denham's part. Training, instinct, desperation, whatever it was that fed the impulse, made him wheel to meet this new threat. There was no doubt in Hayden's mind now that the man intended to shoot and apparently there was none in the minds of the officers.

And so, stunned and powerless to interfere, he simply watched in morbid fascination as the three shots hammered in the room, and he knew instantly the results of that exchange. Denham was an expert of sorts but so were Garvey and Malone. They must have fired a fraction of a second quicker because they stood in their tracks, nothing changing in their faces, ready to shoot again but holding their fire.

Denham took both slugs, one high up in the arm which seemed to recoil. The other apparently struck him in the thigh because the leg started to collapse. He made one final effort to bring the gun to bear but could no longer hold it, and as it dropped from his limp fingers the leg gave way and he fell lopsidedly to the floor.

Hayden was never sure what happened in the next three or four minutes. He had but one thought in mind now, and when he could move he went directly to the divan and sat close to Marion, his arms enveloping her. She came to him immediately, leaning her weight against him, her face buried in the corner of his neck. He could feel her trying to get her breath while her body was racked by small convulsive sobs she could not control. He spoke softly, comforting her, conscious of his own muscular weakness as reaction released the tension that had been punishing him.

"It's all right, sweetheart. It's all over."

He said other things, and he could feel the sobs stop and her breathing grow more regular. When she was ready, she released herself. She brushed the wetness from her cheeks and tried to smile at him.

"I'll behave now."

"You're wonderful," he said. "Are you sure you're all right?"

"I am now."

"Don't you want to go into the bedroom and lie down for a while?"

"I couldn't. Not now. I can't even sit still. Isn't there something I can do?"

"How about making some drinks?" he asked, giving words to the first thought that came to mind.

"No." She stood up and straightened her dress. "But I'll make some coffee."

"Good." He walked part way to the kitchen door with her. "I'll be out in a couple of minutes."

When he looked about he saw that Lieutenant Garvey was just hanging up the telephone. Malone had collected the guns from Freeman and Denham, and he had now hunkered down in front of Denham and was helping straighten the wounded leg as Denham leaned back, his shoulders against the front of the divan.

"There'll be a doctor and an ambulance here in a few minutes," Garvey said.

Denham watched him, his bespectacled eyes painridden and sullen. "You two are quick with your guns," he said morosely, "but you need practice."

"I thought we did pretty well," Garvey said. "We didn't have much time. We don't like to shoot to kill if we can help it." He glanced at Freeman. "How are you, Mr. Freeman? Can you hold on?"

Freeman was sitting in a straight-backed chair, the heel of his left hand pressed beneath the right shoulder. The round face was no longer chalky and stiff, and his eyes were dull and disinterested.

"I think he busted a collarbone but I'm okay. It's a damn good thing you got here when you did. I never even shot a gun before."

"We're all lucky," Hayden said. "What brought you back anyway?"

Garvey considered the question, and for the first time since Hayden had met him he saw the lieutenant smile. It was not a big smile but it was pretty good for Garvey. He seemed pleased about what he had to say.

"Did you think we'd forgotten about the knife, Mr. Hayden?"

"Oh?"

"It took a while but we definitely traced it to you. Without the Lamar woman's statement we had what we call a pretty airtight case against either you or your wife or both."

"Did you ever consider Denham?"

"We considered everybody," Garvey said. "With Denham we had no motive, but in this business when you have the facts to warrant an arrest you make it and let the motive develop later."

He took a moment to glance at the wounded man on the floor before he continued.

"We spent a lot of time on Freeman but we couldn't crack him. He had no reason to take that knife from your house or any opportunity. Neither did Mr. Corbin. It didn't take us long to check him out tonight, and what they told us at Jerry's Tavern was enough to start us thinking in another direction. There wasn't anybody left but Denham and we came back to pick him up.... I still don't know what the motive is, do you?"

"I know," Hayden said, "but it goes 'way back and it's not too easy to understand."

The sound of a siren fading outside took Garvey to the front door, and Hayden moved into the kitchen and swung the door behind him. He moved up beside his wife, who was standing by the sink, and slipped his arm about her waist. Again she leaned her head against his shoulder and he said: "How's the coffee coming?"

"It should be perking any minute."

"How about the baby?"

"He's fine too," she said and digressed with a sigh. "I'm awfully glad it wasn't Ted."

"Me too."

"What will they do to Roger?"

Hayden said he did not know. "He's a lawyer and he's got plenty of money, but from now on it's up to the State's Attorney and the courts. We're not going to worry about Roger and we're not going to worry about us because everything's going to be fine. We'll have a divorce in no time and after that—"

He let the sentence dangle and turned her by the shoulders until she faced him.

"You don't mind marrying me again, do you?"

He saw the answer in her eyes as she put her hands on the back of his neck. She kissed him hard and passionately and almost as quickly stepped back.

"I'd like to, Mr. Hayden."

He grinned at her and then gave her a firm but affectionate slap on the rump as she turned toward the stove. He said they'd probably have to be poor for a couple of years until the insurance money was repaid, and when she said it didn't really matter she sounded as though she meant it.

www.ingramcontent.com/pod-product-compliance
Lightning Source LLC
Chambersburg PA
CBHW011447170626
46816CB00008B/2560